Mollie sat ⟨...⟩ barbecue and tucked her feet under her legs. The swing creaked in protest as she began to rock slowly. "So, Cindy, what's the big problem that's got you all wound up?"

Cindy turned toward her with a troubled frown. "Is it that obvious?"

"It sure is," Mollie replied without hesitation. "It takes a lot to get you uptight. You're our family optimist, remember?"

"The family optimist is sinking fast this time," Cindy lamented, throwing her hands into the air. "I still don't know what to do for my Creative Communication project! If I don't come up with a super idea by class tomorrow morning, Mr. Thomas will pulverize me!"

"Too bad Nicole isn't here," Mollie remarked. "We could always count on her to solve the real brainteasers. Hey, why don't you call her?"

"I could . . ." Cindy's voice trailed off as she considered the idea. "Maybe it will make Nicole feel closer if she has a dilemma from home to ponder."

"Sure, you could call," Mollie coaxed, excited over the prospect of contacting their older sister. "We can both talk to her!"

"Let's go for it!"

The SISTERS Series
by Jennifer Cole
Published by Fawcett Girls Only Books:

*Other titles in the Girls Only series
available upon request*

SISTERS
AND THEN THERE WERE TWO

Jennifer Cole

FAWCETT GIRLS ONLY • NEW YORK

RLI: VL: 5 & up
IL: 6 & up

A Fawcett Girls Only Book
Published by Ballantine Books
Copyright © 1988 by Cloverdale Press, Inc.

Library of Congress Catalog Card Number: 88-91110

ISBN 0-449-13494-6

Printed in Canada

First Edition: October 1988

Chapter 1

*"M*ollie Lewis does it again!" Heather pro-claimed with open admiration.

"Exactly!" Linda chimed in.

"You have the best taste in clothes," Sarah agreed.

"Thanks," Mollie said, glowing under the praise of her best friends as they strolled out of Max-ine's Dress Emporium. The four of them had spent most of Saturday morning at the mall, shopping for new back-to-school outfits. Mollie had been the last one to find an outfit, but managed to find the group's favorite, a pink sundress with just enough ruffle to give it a delicate, feminine touch.

"Let's rest for a few minutes," Heather sug-gested, glancing around the mall full of shoppers. "Over by the fountain."

Mollie shifted her bags from one arm to the other. "Good idea. This stuff I picked up for my mom at the gourmet shop is getting heavy."

The girls weaved through the bustling crowd and plopped down wearily on the circular bench surrounding the large spouting fountain in the center of the huge two-level structure.

"The summer sure flew by fast," Mollie remarked with a sigh.

"It'll be nice to be sophomores, though," Heather pointed out excitedly.

"And it'll be nice to see all of the boys in our class every day," Sarah added. "They're scattered all over the place during vacation, and it's hard to run into them without chasing around all over town."

"You make it sound like we're boy crazy," Linda accused.

"Well, aren't we?" Sarah challenged, setting off a burst of giggles.

"The boys our age seem so childish, though," Mollie blurted out suddenly, causing her friends to gasp in surprise.

"You never felt that way before," Heather said with a frown.

"Who do you have your eye on, Mollie?" Linda wondered. "A junior? A senior?"

"No one in particular," Mollie replied with a shrug. "I guess I'm tired of boys who act like kids."

"Sophomores aren't kids," Sarah objected.

"Who do you think is good-looking, Mollie?" Heather asked.

"Well ..." Mollie's voice trailed off for a moment as she scanned the mall for a hunk. "Look, over there by the computer store. See that dark-haired guy in the gray suit?"

"Yeah," Heather said, wrinkling her nose. "You think he's cute?"

"Definitely," Mollie declared, her pretty face serious.

"He looks like a banker!" Heather judged with a critical eye.

"He's positively ancient!" Linda exclaimed. "For crying out loud, Mollie, he's at least eighteen!"

Mollie tossed her long blond curls over her shoulder and gazed at her friends with an indulgent expression. "Now that I've expanded my horizons, I find mature guys a lot more interesting."

"Expanded what?" Heather snorted.

Mollie sighed with mild exasperation as she faced her puzzled friends. "I'm talking about my trip to Quebec with Nicole and Cindy, of course. Traveling to another country and falling in love with a hockey player who speaks French has changed me forever. I can't turn back the clock and be the silly girl you knew before." Mollie sighed dreamily as a picture of dark, handsome Paul Deniere drifted into her thoughts. She was over him, but she would never forget her first real love.

"Don't you think 'falling in love' is a little strong?" Linda asked doubtfully.

"Falling for a sports figure like Paul is called a crush," Heather stated with authority. "I should know. I had a crush on Joe Montana for four whole months last year."

"Mollie's kidding us," Sarah said with a knowing gleam in her eye. "She only wishes she was a jump ahead of us in the romance department."

The three of them began to laugh.

"You really had us going there for a minute," Heather said, "but let's face it. We're only fifteen years old. All our major kissing happens in our daydreams."

Mollie's round blue eyes flashed with hurt, but the girls were too busy gabbing to notice. Her own friends were laughing at her! She knew she could lose her temper and lay it on the line. But it wouldn't make them understand. You've either experienced first love or you haven't. Suddenly Heather, Linda, and Sarah seemed incredibly immature.

"What should we do now?" Heather asked lightly, unaware of Mollie's irritation. "Eat lunch?"

"Okay," Linda agreed. "Let's have hamburgers."

"We'd better have a salad if we want our new clothes to fit on Monday," Sarah said.

"Especially you, Linda," Heather teased. "You had to lie down on the dressing room floor to zip up your pastel jeans."

"I bought the next size," Linda shot back hotly.

The girls bickered all the way to the Salad Bowl. Mollie went along with a stiff smile, eager for the shopping trip to end.

Cindy Lewis was tossing slices of bread onto the table in two crooked rows an hour later when Mollie burst into the kitchen like a funnel cloud.

"Having a late lunch or early dinner?" Mollie gibed, referring to her sixteen-year-old sister's healthy appetite.

"Aren't we in a wonderful mood?" Cindy shot back with a teasing grin. "Trouble at the mall?"

"Trouble with my silly friends," Mollie exclaimed in disgust.

"What did they do? Go for a dip in the fountain?"

"I could've handled that," Mollie retorted, opening the refrigerator. "It's no crime to grab the limelight once in a while."

"Yeah, right," Cindy said. She was well aware that her younger sister and her friends liked to grab the limelight as often as possible. "So, what's wrong?"

"Heather, Linda, and Sarah don't understand me anymore," Mollie wailed, flipping open a can of diet pop.

"Bologna," Cindy said, snapping her fingers.

"Baloney?" Mollie repeated. "My life is nuked, and all you can say is baloney?"

"Mollie—"

"Oh, how I wish Nicole hadn't dropped this family like a hot potato and run off to a college in Boston," Mollie lamented, taking a swig of pop. "Bring a problem to Nicole, and she sympathizes! She solves it!"

"Mollie," Cindy began again, "I need bologna for my sandwiches. As long as you're standing at the refrigerator . . ."

"Oh, sorry." Mollie sheepishly handed Cindy two packages of lunch meat.

"Get the mayonnaise and mustard, too, will ya?"

Mollie obeyed and set the jars on the table.

"Thanks." Cindy began to spread the mayonnaise on the bread. "You know as well as I do that Nicole didn't drop us and run off. She belongs at a college back East."

"But I need help, and she's gone," Mollie complained. "And I suppose you're going off surfing with all of your wonderful friends."

"The sandwiches gave me away, right?"

Mollie sank into a chair with a heavy sigh.

"Mollie, tell me what's going on," Cindy coaxed. "I'll try to help out like Nicole used to. Really I will."

"Okay." Mollie propped her chin on her hand as if the weight of the world rested heavily on her. "I think I'm growing away from my friends."

"Oh, Mollie, it can't be true." Cindy dropped into a chair beside her, waving her kitchen knife in protest.

Mollie nodded her blond head sadly. "It was horrible today, Cindy. They actually laughed at me."

Cindy stared blankly at her forlorn sister. She'd been expecting a small crisis like a disagreement over a shade of nail polish. She suddenly realized that she wasn't going to slide into Nicole's shoes effortlessly. Glib advice always seemed to pop off the top of Nicole's lovely brown head—often laced with a French phrase or two. Unfortunately nothing especially witty was popping into Cindy's head at the moment.

"I can't believe how babyish they are," Mollie rambled on resentfully. "The worst part of all is that they think that my love for Paul was nothing but a silly crush."

"That's rough," Cindy agreed, tapping the dull knife against her left hand, leaving a glob of mayonnaise on her palm. "Ugh!" she exclaimed.

"Are you tuned into my problem or not?" Mollie demanded.

Cindy hastily wiped her hand with a napkin. "I'm trying to help."

"Paul was my first true love! Not a kiddie crush like they think."

"I know that. But you're the first one of your friends to really fall in love," Cindy consoled, "so naturally you've taken a step ahead. You can't automatically expect them to understand how you feel."

"They shouldn't have laughed."

"No, but your group is known to burst into giggles without much reason. Maybe you're taking it too seriously."

"I'm really hurting, Cindy," Mollie said with a sniff. "Nicole would know what to do."

"Maybe she would," Cindy agreed. "I sure don't."

"Don't you miss Nicole as much as I do?" Mollie asked.

"Sure I do," Cindy admitted. "But moping around isn't going to do either of us any good. All we can do is try to help each other out."

"You're right," Mollie said. She paused thoughtfully. "Hey Cindy, if you really mean that, would you mind if I hung out with you and your friends at the beach this afternoon?"

"Why?" Cindy asked in surprise. She stood up and began to slap bologna on the slices of bread.

"I'm ready for a change, I guess."

"It must have been a bad scene this morning." Cindy cast a worried frown at her impetuous sister. "You're welcome to join us, but I'll have to meet you there. I had some errands to do for Mom this morning, so I'm already late."

"That's okay," Mollie assured her. "You go ahead.

It might take me a while to get ready anyway."
With a new spring in her step, she headed upstairs to change.

"Mollie's coming to the beach especially to hang
out with us?" Grant MacPhearson asked Cindy
later as they sat side by side on the gang's beach
blanket. Grant had been dating Cindy for just
about a year now and was very familiar with the
huge differences between the Lewis sisters.

Cindy looked into Grant's puzzled blue-green
eyes, then glanced around the blanket to find all
her friends reeling from her announcement. "I
know it seems strange...."

"I'll say," Carey remarked. "Mollie usually comes
to the beach to chase guys, not waves."

"Is she trying to sell us something?" Anna wondered aloud.

Duffy shook his bright red head. "Those fluo-
rescent lights in the stores have finally fried the
supershopper's brain!"

"Mollie's going through a rough time right now,"
Cindy explained as she rubbed some bright pink
zinc oxide on her nose. "She's missing Nicole a
lot, and to top it all off, she says her friends don't
understand her anymore...." Cindy trailed off,
flashing Duffy a hopeful expression.

"What are you looking at me for?" Duffy demanded.

"I hope you'll control your wisecracks, Duffy,"
Cindy said, accustomed to being blunt with her
rambunctious childhood friend. "Mollie's pretty
sensitive right now."

"Give me a break, Lewis," Duffy shot back. "I'm
a nice guy."

His last remark caused gales of laughter to erupt on the crowded beach blanket.

"Here comes the Lewis mobile," Grant observed, pointing to the parking lot. Moments later the Lewises' station wagon rolled to a stop on the blacktop, and Mollie hopped out of the passenger side of the car dressed in a purple terry cloth sunsuit, her long blond hair gathered up in a ponytail, and huge sunglasses perched on her nose. Cindy immediately jumped up and waved her arms in the air to attract Mollie's attention. Mollie waved back and began to scamper across the sand toward them.

"Hi, everybody!" Mollie greeted the group brightly, sitting down on the only vacant corner of the blanket. "Looks like a lot of awesome waves out there," she observed in an effort to sound like part of the surfer crowd.

"Very, very awesome," Duffy agreed.

"They close the mall for repairs?" Grant asked with a devilish grin.

"I was there this morning, and the building was in pretty good shape," Mollie tossed back lightly, determined to show them how nice and fun she could be.

"I figured you'd wear a swimsuit," Cindy said in surprise.

"I don't feel like swimming today," Mollie explained. "I just thought I'd stop by to hang out with the best juniors at Vista High for a while."

Mollie's compliment hit its mark, bringing smiles to everyone's lips.

"You've got some real sense for a sophomore," Duffy said.

"You're wearing a cute outfit, Mollie," Anna complimented.

Carey nodded. "Purple is a good color on you."

Mollie glowed under their praise, struggling not to appear too eager. She wondered why she'd never bothered with Cindy's friends before. They really were nice.

"When are you going to ride your first curl, Mollie?" Grant asked, reaching to the Lewises' cooler for a sandwich.

"Catch a wave, and you're sittin' on top of the world," Duffy chimed in.

"Curl. Wave. Sounds like beauty salon talk," Mollie said.

"Take that back or I'll bury you in the sand," Duffy threatened.

"I'm only kidding," Mollie hastened to assure them. "As a matter of fact, I figure it's about time I learned to surf."

The crowd didn't bother to hide their amazement.

"But, Mollie," Cindy objected, "surfing isn't as easy as it looks."

Mollie brushed aside her sister's objection with a carefree hand. "I can handle it, Cindy—if you're willing to teach me, that is."

Cindy looked into Mollie's anxious blue eyes, and all of her arguments melted away. "All right. We'll give it a shot next weekend."

Cindy was surrounded with good-humored but skeptical looks.

"This is going to work out great!" Mollie said, pushing her glasses up on her nose. She had never thought she'd have a better time at the beach than she did at the mall!

Chapter 2

"**S**top, Mom!" *Mollie exclaimed, flouncing into* the kitchen in her ruffled pink sundress. "Don't hang up the phone!" She hastily dumped her schoolbooks and purse on the kitchen counter in a heap and dashed over to her mother, who was standing across the room holding the telephone receiver.

Laura Lewis gasped in surprise as Mollie headed across the linoleum in her direction, teetering precariously in a pair of high-heeled woven-leather sandals. She replaced the receiver on the hook just in time to catch her youngest daughter in midflight.

"You were talking to Nicole," Mollie accused, her round blue eyes wide with drama. "You hung up before I had a chance to say anything!"

Mrs. Lewis gazed down at her petite daughter and gave her a mild shake. "Simmer down, Mollie. I'm catering a luncheon art lecture at the Santa

11

Barbara Museum of Art tomorrow and was tracking down some jumbo shrimp."

"Oh. Sorry, Mom, guess I got carried away. It's just that we haven't heard from Nicole since last week, and now it's Thursday already. Don't ya think she should have called by now?" Mollie asked.

"She'll call, don't worry. She's probably just busy getting used to college life."

"Nicole would never call at this time of the day anyway," Mrs. Lewis pointed out logically. "She knows that Cindy has swim practice after school and your father won't be home until this evening."

"You're right," Mollie admitted with a heavy sigh, tossing her long blond hair behind her shoulders.

"How about a snack?" Mrs. Lewis offered. She pointed to the apple pie on the table. "We had an extra one left over at the shop, so I brought it home for a special treat."

"No, I better not," Mollie declined, eyeing the pie longingly. Mrs. Lewis ran her own catering business, Moveable Feasts, and her creations were out of this world. It was taking all of Mollie's willpower to turn down the pie. "I'm on a new diet. I stuffed myself at Nicole's going-away party and gained two whole pounds!'

"Perhaps you'll change your mind after dinner," Mrs. Lewis said.

Mollie shrugged. "Well, I'm going upstairs for now. I bought a new beauty magazine to look over. I promised Anna I'd find just the right makeover for her."

"Anna?" her mother questioned in surprise. "She's Cindy's friend."

"She's my friend, too," Mollie explained in a slightly defensive tone.

"Since when?"

"Since the weekend. I've been hanging out a lot with Cindy and her crowd. They've really welcomed me into the group. Sometimes I even forget that I'm only a sophomore. I feel like I'm a junior, just like they are."

Concern crossed her mother's face. "What about Heather and Sarah and Linda?" she asked. "Last year you girls were inseparable."

"It seems like a million years ago, Mom. Things have changed—I've changed. Falling in love with Paul in Quebec during the summer put sort of a barrier of maturity between my friends and me. They seem so juvenile, so—so . . ."

"So sophomoric," Mrs. Lewis supplied dryly.

"See, you do understand," Mollie declared. She gave her mother a quick hug and turned to scoop up her belongings from the counter.

"Say, young lady, aren't you wearing Nicole's sandals?" Mrs. Lewis demanded suddenly, as Mollie began to teeter her way along once again. "They look two sizes too large for you."

"Oui," Mollie replied with a giggle, imitating Nicole's French responses. "I'm sure she left them behind on purpose. They're much more my style than hers anyway."

"Scoot!" Mrs. Lewis waved her on in exasperation.

"Au revoir!"

*   *   *

When Cindy Lewis exited Vista High later that afternoon, Grant was sitting on the concrete steps waiting for her.

"Hey, hunk," she said in a low, sultry tone as she walked up behind him.

Grant stood up and turned his dark, curly head to face her. "Oh, it's only you," he teased, his eyes full of mischief.

They headed for the student parking lot arm in arm, their jean-clad legs casting long shadows on the blacktop. Grant's bright red Trans Am was easy to spot from a distance, gleaming like fire in the Santa Barbara sunshine.

"So, how is Vista's champion swimmer?" Grant asked.

"Okay," Cindy replied with a slight scowl. "Coach Lawford is such a taskmaster. All he did today was march from lane to lane ranting and raving about beach bums and soft summer flab."

"He sure couldn't have been talking about his champion freestyler," Grant consoled, giving her arm a squeeze. "You're in perfect shape, Cindy. You didn't let up all summer long—surfing, jogging, tennis—"

Cindy's burst of laughter interrupted his glowing tribute. "Thanks, my ego is inflated once again to its normal size. Now, tell me about your first staff meeting for the yearbook."

Grant cleared his throat and adjusted an imaginary tie at the collar of his red knit shirt. "Sports editor Grant MacPhearson was welcomed to the staff with a hearty round of applause. . . ."

Cindy elbowed him sharply below the rib cage.

"I'm serious, Grant. Being sports editor is an important position on the yearbook."

"Sure, to a jock like you it would be," Grant teased. When Cindy didn't laugh, he took on a serious tone. "I know how important sports coverage is to you, Cin. That's one reason I went for that particular position on the staff. I can get some hands-on training in journalism and hang around the pool to watch you at the same time."

When they reached the Trans Am, Grant swiftly unlocked the doors, and they tossed their belongings in the back seat. Within minutes they were on the road, headed for Cindy's neighborhood of well-kept lawns and neatly clipped shrubbery.

"Another smart move you made last spring was suggesting that we take the creative communication course together."

"I guess that was my idea," Grant recalled, flashing Cindy a smile as he stopped at a red light. "I think some of our arguments in the past could've been avoided if we'd communicated better."

"It was doubly brilliant because it's turned out to be our only class together this semester," Cindy added with a laugh.

A few minutes later Grant pulled his Trans Am up the driveway leading to the Lewises' Spanish-style home.

"Looks like our little mascot is waiting for us," Grant observed, shutting off the engine. He gestured to the front step where Mollie sat with Cinders, the cat, in her lap and a set of headphones clamped around her head.

"I wonder what she's up to." Cindy said. "I

didn't realize when I invited her to hang out with us on Saturday that it was an open invitation."

"Whatever makes you say that?" Grant remarked good-naturedly. "Just because she sat at our lunch table every day this week?"

"I hope no one thinks she's a problem," Cindy said suddenly, her green eyes glowing anxiously. "Has anyone said anything to you?"

"No, no, of course not." Grant shook his dark head, waving at Mollie as she scurried across the lawn in their direction. She'd abandoned the headphones but was still holding Cinders. "I'm just surprised that she's latched on to you—to our gang. You and Mollie have such different personalities. She's the type of girl who could spend an hour painting her fingernails. You're the type of girl who could play a set of tennis, wash three cars, and jog two miles in the same amount of time."

Cindy couldn't deny it. It was a well-known fact that the three Lewis sisters were distinctly different, each having friends of her own. But they were in the habit of uniting during times of trouble. And losing Nicole to a faraway college just naturally seemed like a time to draw together.

"Hi!" Mollie greeted them cheerfully. She set Cinders down on the driveway, and the cat romped nearby in the grass. "I thought you'd never get here!" she exclaimed, resting her arms on the edge of Grant's open car window.

"Why, what's going on?" Cindy asked, twisting in the bucket seat to grab her nylon bag from the back.

"Nothing, really," Mollie admitted. "It's just kind

of quiet around here. I've already finished my magazine." She studied Cindy's face, making her sister squirm uneasily. "You know, Cin, my magazine has an article on the benefits of facials. You should have one. All that sun and salt air on the beach is wrecking your complexion—Anna's and Carey's, too."

"We protect our skin," Cindy declared. "I always use suntan lotion, and zinc oxide on my nose."

"Hah! Just feel my cheek, Grant," Mollie invited, lowering her face close to his.

"Mollie!" Cindy scolded sharply.

Grant touched her cheek, looking a bit uncomfortable. "Yeah. It's soft, Mollie," he said, clearing his throat.

With a pointed glance at her sister, Mollie straightened up again and picked up Cinders. "What did I tell you? Nicole's not the only one in this family who gives good advice. And since she's all the way across the country, we have only each other to rely on."

She crossed the lawn toward the house singing in carefree abandon.

"Let me check out your cheek," Grant murmured, kissing Cindy lightly.

"How is it?"

"Mmm ... perfect."

Cindy snuggled up beside him. "Now this is what I call creative communication."

Chapter 3

*T*he phone rang while Cindy was loading the dishwasher that evening. She quickly dried her hands on a towel near the sink and picked up the receiver. "Hello?"

"Bonsoir ma chère soeur!"

"Nicole!" Cindy exclaimed with pleasure. "It's about time you called!"

"Are you in the middle of dinner?" Nicole asked.

"No. We're finished. Mom and Dad are out shopping, and I'm cleaning up the kitchen."

"Where's Mollie?"

Cindy sighed and dropped into a kitchen chair. "She is supposed to be helping me, but she went to the laundry room in search of some new rubber gloves—ten minutes ago!"

"That's typical," Nicole replied with a laugh. "Mollie will make up any excuse to get out of doing chores."

"Too right," Cindy agreed. "So tell me, Nicole, what's college like?"

"It's okay," Nicole said, then quickly added, "So what's new at home?"

Cindy immediately detected an awkward note in her sister's voice. "Nicole, is something wrong? This is me, Cindy, remember? You can tell me anything."

The line was silent for a long moment. "Well, actually, Cindy, everyone expects me to be like . . . you."

"What do you mean?" Cindy asked. She couldn't figure out why on earth anyone would want *Nicole* to be like *her*—more likely the other way around.

"A quintessential California girl," Nicole blurted out in frustration. "You know, sun-bleached hair, a rock-hard body, tanned skin, and a surfboard balanced over my head."

Cindy unconsciously reached for her short, streaked hair and looked down at her dark, lean legs, stretched out comfortably and crossed at the ankles. She understood Nicole's problem now and felt a sudden wave of compassion for her eighteen-year-old sister. Nicole certainly didn't live up to the sporty California-girl image. Her passion was French culture, not beach culture.

"You should've told everyone you were a French foreign exchange student," Cindy teased, hoping to lift Nicole's spirits. "They'd treat you like a celebrity."

Nicole laughed in spite of herself. "Thanks for the advice, Cin, but I don't think I'd pass. I've never even been to France."

"So? Big deal," Cindy said lightly. "You just

have to get out there and try to fit in. You can dazzle them if you try."

"I have been trying," Nicole insisted. "I went out with a group on campus last night."

"How was it?"

"Disaster!" Nicole lamented. "As soon as they found out that I was from Santa Barbara, they began to bombard me with questions about impact zones and nose diving."

Cindy giggled. "Nose riding, not nose diving. It's when a surfer stands on the very front of the surfboard."

"I'll bet a lot of them do nose dives standing on the edge like that," Nicole shot back defensively.

"That's a good point," Cindy agreed.

"Seriously, Cindy. I don't know what to do. You can't possibly imagine how tough it is to be a college freshman. It's like being an awkward little kid all over again. At Vista last year I was on top of everything. The kids respected me just as I was." Nicole paused. "Now, all of a sudden, *I'm* a new kid here, and I don't feel like I measure up."

Cindy couldn't believe that college was turning her confident, controlled sister into a chicken. I guess she had reason to be nervous about going away to college, Cindy thought, recalling her sister's unusual behavior just before she'd left for Briarwood College. Until then Cindy had thought of Nicole as the most together person she knew. She still felt funny giving advice to her older sister.

"I'm sure next week you'll be the most popular girl on campus," Cindy comforted. "Just try to keep cool."

"I'm trying to." Nicole gave a strained laugh. "Do you know, I even considered bleaching my hair so I'd look more like a California girl?"

"Somehow, Nicole, I don't think you'd look good as a blonde. It's just not you," Cindy remarked. "Besides, the Nicole Lewis I know and love can take the pressure."

"But—"

Cindy cut her off. "The real Nicole Lewis found work in the competitive world of fashion modeling. The real Nicole Lewis ran Moveable Feasts while Mom was recovering from surgery—and disposed of a zillion crates of mushrooms in a tax-deductible way! Can't you see that trying to act like a beach bunny will only drag you down? And what about your classes? You're loving art history and French literature. That certainly beats living in a Gidget-goes-to-Boston movie."

Nicole sighed deeply. *"Merci,"* she finally murmured. "I needed a pep talk from you."

"Just be yourself," Cindy advised.

Mollie burst into the room all of a sudden, carrying a pair of orange rubber gloves. "Is that Nicole on the line?" she demanded excitedly.

Cindy nodded, then spoke to Nicole again. "Mollie is anxious to talk to you, so I'll say good-bye."

"Oh, by the way, Cindy," Nicole said on a final note, "have you seen my favorite leather sandals? You know, the ones with the high wooden heels? I was wondering if I might have left them lying around in the rush to pack."

Cindy was well aware of the fact that Mollie had worn them to school that very day, but didn't want to add to Nicole's misery. "I don't know where they are, exactly," she hedged. "Here's Mollie."

Mollie grabbed the phone from Cindy's hand and tossed the rubber gloves into Cindy's lap. "Nicole, it's about time you checked in!" Mollie began to pace across the floor, listening intently. "Sandals?"

Cindy shot Mollie a pleased smirk as her younger sister paled.

"Gee, I guess I have seen them some place.... Aren't they a little immature-looking for a college coed?"

Cindy chuckled softly, only to receive a lethal glare from Mollie.

"Okay, Nicole. I'll tell Mom to mail them to you. What's new here? Oh, well I'm on a new diet! I'm totally into fiber ... Oh, you know, whole grains, fruits and vegetables. I feel so healthy. Maybe you should try changing your diet.... Okay, okay, just trying to help."

Cindy fidgeted in her chair impatiently as Mollie continued chatting. Finally, with an exasperated breath, she placed the rubber gloves in Mollie's free hand and left Mollie to muddle through her share of the dishes alone.

"So, here you are, Mollie!" Heather exclaimed. "This is the last place I expected to run into you. Especially after school!"

Mollie was seated at one of the sewing machines in the back of the huge deserted home economics room. She smiled tightly over the spool holder. "Hi, Heather," she said, clearing her throat nervously.

"What gives, anyway?" Heather demanded, her heels echoing in the silence as she walked purposefully toward Mollie.

Mollie concentrated intensely on the wrinkled cotton print positioned on the machine's throat plate, silently scolding herself. She had successfully dodged Heather, as well as Linda and Sarah, for the whole week, never having to say more than hello in the hallway. And now, on Friday afternoon after school hours, she had allowed Heather to corner her for a heart-to-heart chat. If only she hadn't flubbed up the collar on her sewing project during class that morning, she'd have been on her way home by now and out of Heather's reach.

"Mollie, what gives?" Heather repeated impatiently, now standing over Mollie with a grim expression.

Mollie laughed without humor. "I have to finish this halter top by four-thirty. Boy, oh, boy, have I ever messed it up! The collar is all wrong. I've sewn it on twice and ripped it off twice. It just doesn't fit right. Oh, who ever heard of putting a collar on a halter anyway?"

Heather looked down at the hole-speckled fabric. Even though Mollie knew she had taken the same class last year and was a whiz at sewing, she showed no trace of sympathy, nor did she offer to help. "That's not what I'm talking about, Mollie, and I think you know it. The other girls and I have barely seen you all week. You didn't eat once at our lunch table, and you never call any of us anymore."

"I waved at you yesterday, Heather," Mollie

reminded her, "right after third period. You were coming out of the gym and I was—"

"Big deal!" Heather scoffed in a hurt tone. "Did we do something to make you mad?"

"No, no, of course not," Mollie hastily assured her.

"Well, if we're imagining things, I'm sorry," Heather said, brightening. "Linda, Sarah, and I are going over to the amusement park tomorrow. The place is crawling with guys on a Saturday afternoon." A mischievous grin spread over her face. "Can we count you in?"

Mollie broke away from Heather's straightforward gaze and busily fumbled with the presser foot on the machine. "Gee, Heather, I'm sure it will be thrilling for all of you...."

"Thrilling for us?" Heather gasped in surprise. "Since when are you above going to amusement parks? We had to tear you off the roller coaster a couple of months ago because your face was turning green—after five rides!"

"That was ages ago," Mollie claimed with uncharacteristic dignity. "And besides, I already have plans for tomorrow. Cindy and her friends have invited me to one of their beach bashes. I can't let them down."

"I don't understand you, Mollie. All of a sudden you're trailing after Cindy. What's wrong with us?"

"Nothing," Mollie replied, still pretending to concentrate on her sewing. "It's just that since Nicole is away, Cindy and I really have to stick together."

Heather rolled her eyes in obvious disgust. "It'll never last," she predicted. "You and Cindy have nothing in common, except your parents, of course, and your dog and cats."

"Oh, yeah?" Mollie snapped. "Cindy's dying to give me surfing lessons, and I'm dying to try it".

"Hah! You're not the type, Mollie," Heather judged smugly. "Knowing how to swim isn't enough to prepare you for surfing. Cindy is in peak condition."

"I look pretty good on the beach," Mollie contended, "especially in a bikini."

"I'm talking about a fitness program, dummy. Your idea of exercise is to shop till you drop. Cindy jogs every day—for fun!"

"You're not even trying to understand," Mollie accused in a self-pitying tone.

"I understand, all right," Heather claimed. "You've lost your marbles." Heather turned on her heel and stalked off.

Mollie shrugged and continued to struggle with the sewing machine. *I can't help it if Heather's mad at me,* she thought. *I didn't want to hurt her or the others. But let's face it, I've outgrown them.* She looked down at the crumpled material in front of her. *If I don't finish this dumb halter top soon, I'll outgrow this too—even before it's done!*

Chapter 4

$\mathcal{I}$t was Cindy's habit to rise early on Saturdays and get the morning started with a jog along the beach. This Saturday was no exception. By seven o'clock she was dressed in her lavender sweat suit and Reeboks, with wrist weights in place. She paused at the dresser to run a comb through her short sun-bleached hair, then headed for the garage to pick up Winston, the Lewises' big black Newfoundland dog. Within minutes they were trotting down the driveway together at an easy pace.

Before long they'd reached the shores of the Pacific Ocean. Cindy loved the sea at this time of day with the seagulls and Winston her only company. The atmosphere was peaceful, the air crisp, with a tinge of salt. Cindy moved along the shoreline behind Winston, her shoes making their mark in the sand beside the dog's huge paw prints. Cindy looked out to sea, inhaling with deep contentment. She watched the waves swell in the distance, then roll into shore, dissolving into white foam on the saturated sand. It looked like a perfect day for surfing. Sometimes Cindy imagined herself living right on the beach in a small hut, living and breathing to surf. Of course she'd have time for Grant, too. They could live to surf together. . . .

Winston's bark drew her back to reality. He was circling a large rock ahead, seaweed on his nose.

"Party time's over, boy." She laughed, pulling the wet green weeds from his face. "Let's head back for breakfast."

"Good morning," Mrs. Lewis greeted cheerfully as Cindy bounced through the back door with energy to spare. "Have a nice jog?"

"Super." Cindy took a glass from the cupboard and poured herself some orange juice from the plastic pitcher on the table.

"I talked to Nicole a few minutes ago," Mrs. Lewis said, putting a dab of butter in the omelet pan on the stove.

"Oh, really? How is she?" Cindy asked casually, pulling up a chair.

"She sounded sort of down," Mrs. Lewis said with a frown.

"I'm sure she's just homesick," Cindy hedged, not about to betray her sister's confidence.

Mrs. Lewis nodded slowly. "College is a big step."

"Can I have the first omelet? I'm starving."

"I suppose so. I'm trying a new recipe with garlic and red peppers."

"Go light on the breath killers," Cindy exclaimed. "I'm meeting the gang at the beach later."

Mrs. Lewis cracked some eggs in her mixing bowl and carried the shells to the waste basket beside the broom closet. "What in the world is this?" she asked, pulling a piece of wrinkled floral fabric out from behind the basket.

"I don't know," Cindy replied, slipping off her wrist weights. "Looks like a rag or something."

"It's some kind of halter top," Mrs. Lewis decided after careful examination. "A hand-sewn one, to be sure."

"Looks like a hand-sewn disaster," Cindy judged, taking a sip of juice.

"That's right!" Mollie said from the doorway. "It is a disaster!" She'd obviously just rolled out of bed. Her long blond hair was fuzzy in the back, her face was free of makeup, and she was still dressed in her Garfield nightshirt. "It's a *C*-minus to be exact!" Mollie grabbed the top from her mother's hands and balled it up in a fit of rage, jamming it into the basket with an accuracy she'd lacked the first time.

"Is this the sewing project you worked on all week?" Mrs. Lewis asked in amazement.

"Yes," Mollie admitted, biting her lower lip.

"Good thing you're a mall hound, Mollie," Cindy teased. "You'd never survive if you actually had to wear the clothes you make!"

"We only had one crummy week to put all the pieces to that crazy halter together," Mollie shot back defensively. "Mrs. Young was testing our sewing skills before assigning us our big projects."

"You would've had better luck trying to fix up

Humpty-Dumpty," Cindy observed over the rim of her glass.

"I did one of the worst jobs in the entire class," Mollie muttered. "I even stayed after school yesterday to finish it. But it wasn't any use. I'll be lucky if Mrs. Young lets me thread needles for the rest of the girls."

"That's a shame, Mollie," Mrs. Lewis consoled, giving her shoulders a squeeze.

"It's too bad, kid," Cindy chimed in. "You do have a flair for fashion. You'd probably have some good ideas to contribute."

"You should have asked Heather for help," Mrs. Lewis reprimanded gently. "A few seams and tucks in the right places couldn've put you on the track."

"She could've helped me," Mollie declared in a self-pitying tone, omitting the fact that she had been dodging her good friend all week long. "She came by the home ec room yesterday afternoon, but she chose to stand by and let me suffer instead!" Mollie retreated in a whirlwind, her blond hair flying in her wake.

"That's an unusual story," Mrs. Lewis pondered.

"Mollie's an unusual girl," Cindy added, pouring herself more juice.

"You know, Cindy, I'm even more concerned about Mollie than I am about Nicole. She just hasn't been herself lately. She was telling me the other day that her friends seem so immature. You don't think she's dropped them completely, do you?"

Cindy shrugged. "Well, I know there is trouble, but I don't know if it's reached the breaking point yet. The way Mollie talks, it's as if Heather and the others are residents of Sesame Street."

"The idea that Mollie has outgrown those girls is ridiculous," Mrs. Lewis scoffed.

"Totally outrageous," Cindy agreed whole-heartedly.

"I suppose she plans to go to the beach with you today," Mrs. Lewis said with a sigh.

"Yeah, she wants to learn how to surf."

"Look out for her," Mrs. Lewis warned. "She's not as strong a swimmer as you are!"

"I figure she'll wipe out with a *C*-minus and head back before noon," Cindy consoled.

"I hope you're right." Mrs. Lewis sighed.

"Be prepared to welcome her home with a diet soda, and a stack of *Beauty Digest* magazines."

Mollie joined Cindy out in the driveway at mid-morning, just as her older sister was strapping her surfboard to her bicycle.

"I'm ready," Mollie announced, proudly display-ing the skimpy string bikini partly hidden under her lacy white coverup.

Cindy straightened up, placed her hands on her slender hips, and inspected Mollie's appear-ance. "What are you ready for?" she asked in a disapproving tone. "A poolside party in Beverly Hills?"

"My surfing lesson, of course," Mollie fired back, setting her mouth in a pout.

"A surfer is much better off wearing a practical swimsuit." Cindy lifted her pink T-shirt up a couple of inches to reveal her blue tank suit underneath.

"I'd look horrible in something like that," Mollie blurted out without thinking. "Not that you do, Cindy," she hastily added, blushing.

"Surfing involves your full concentration," Cindy warned, climbing onto her bicycle. "Pulling and tugging at a skimpy suit like that one could easily upset your timing."

"I'll manage somehow," Mollie said, her fluffy blond ponytail bouncing as she nodded confidently.

The beach was already cluttered with sun worshipers when the Lewis sisters arrived. They parked their bikes at the lifeguard station, collected their belongings, and ran through the hot sand toward their friends, using Duffy Duncan's head of bright red hair as a marker.

"Hi, everybody!" Cindy said, pulling off her shirt and shorts to reveal her trim, athletic body in her blue tank suit. She dropped down on the beach blanket beside Anna and Carey, and Mollie followed suit. "Is Grant here yet?"

"He just hit the water," Anna replied, pointing at his broad shoulders off in the distance.

Cindy spotted Grant just as he was sliding stomach-first onto his board.

"Watching that guy surf is almost as good as doing it yourself," Duffy remarked with admiration, sitting on the edge of the blanket near Cindy.

"I know," Cindy agreed, proud of her boyfriend.

The group watched intently as Grant moved out to sea, his powerful arms digging into the water with smooth, even strokes. He soon joined several other surfers at the surf line, where they were already sitting on their boards waiting for a good breaker. Cindy was with him in spirit, knowing exactly which wave he would catch. Sure enough, when the powerful green cylinder rolled forward feathering with foam, Grant brought one leg up under his chin, then the other, landing on the balls of his feet in the center of the board. He leaned back, tilting the board slightly, making a sharp cut across the wave look effortless.

"What a carver!" Duffy exclaimed.

"Looks easy enough," Mollie piped up, causing everybody to glance at her with surprise.

"I hear you're going to be proving yourself today, kid," Duffy said, winking at the other girls.

"She'll teach us a thing or two," Carey predicted, her eyes dancing with amusement.

"All she needs is a surfboard," Anna put in.

Grant shimmied in smoothly, landing near the crowd with amazing accuracy. He stabbed his board into the sand and plopped down beside Cindy, splattering water on her.

"Ugh!" she cried.

"That's no way to say hello," Grant teased, giving her a salty kiss.

"Great job," Cindy said, now grinning.

"You're just as good," Grant assured her. "Now you can put on a show for me."

"But what about my lesson?" Mollie demanded. She stood up on the beach blanket, slipped off her lacy coverup, and posed in her bikini with a guileless expression.

"Mollie, we have all day for that," Cindy said.

"Well, what's wrong with now?" Mollie pressed.

"Mollie, I—"

"Go on, Cindy," Duffy interrupted. "Mollie can even borrow my board so you can demonstrate on yours. We'll all stay here and watch."

Cindy caught the twinkle in her friend's eye, but Mollie had obviously missed it.

"Thanks, Duffy," she squealed. "Maybe you don't deserve your reputation after all."

"What reputation?"

"Oh, you know, silly. Everyone knows Duffy Duncan will do anything for a laugh."

"Hey, now just a minute!" Duffy rose to his full height in mock anger.

"It's true," Mollie said, lifting the board into the air. In her haste she almost whacked several heads.

"Hit the surf, not my friends," Cindy shouted, her blue-green eyes flashing with anger.

"Lighten up, Cin!" Mollie called, scampering ahead.

Cindy reluctantly rose and picked up her surf-board.

"Give it your best shot, teach," Duffy teased, giving Cindy the thumbs-up signal.

"Your bravery will go down in the history books," Anna predicted dryly.

"We salute you, soldier," Grant added, snapping a stiff hand to his forehead.

Mollie turned out to be more cooperative than Cindy had anticipated. After only a couple of attempts she managed to slide her stomach onto the board, followed by her legs. She paddled easily through the water, cupping her hands just as Cindy had instructed.

"Maybe you should ride the first wave on your stomach," Cindy suggested as they sat side by side on their boards at the surf-line.

"No!" Mollie said firmly. "You explained how to stand, and I've watched you do it a million times!"

"All right," Cindy gave in, noting that some mild swells were forming behind them. "Get ready. And remember what I told you about keeping your weight centered—"

"Hush!"

Cindy rose to her feet and easily maneuvered on the mild rolling wave. To her amazement, Mollie, though shaky, was on her feet as well.

"Look at me! Look at me!" Mollie squealed. Sure enough, the youngest Lewis had followed her sister's instructions. Her arms were extended to maintain good balance and her knees bent slightly to absorb the shock of the wave.

Cindy's friends were standing on shore, applauding like crazy.

Then it was all over. One second Mollie's arms were extended in a balance position, the next they were groping at her loose bikini top. Duffy's board somersaulted and Mollie was tossed through the air, landing in the water with a splash.

"Mollie!" Cindy screamed, diving into the water after her sister.

When Cindy popped back to the surface, her surfboard was within reach, and Mollie was treading water a short distance away. Cindy quickly retrieved her board and pushed it toward Mollie. "Climb onto my board, Mollie!" she ordered anxiously. "Ride in on your stomach while I go find Duffy's board."

"I can't!" Mollie shouted breathlessly. "My top is gone!"

Chapter 5

*"**I** told you so!"* Cindy couldn't resist chiding as she and Mollie struggled in the water. She slid onto her surfboard and sat up, dangling her feet over the sides. "I warned you not to go surfing in that handful of yellow strings."

Mollie swam up to Cindy and clung to the edge of the surfboard, causing it to teeter slightly. "Don't chew me out at time like this," she begged with a sniff.

"Well, I see Duffy's board made it back to shore, anyway," Cindy observed as she focused on the shoreline.

"Tell me what's happening," Mollie insisted. "I can't see anything from down here."

"Duffy is running into the shallow water to pick up his board...." Cindy reported, shielding her eyes against the bright sun with one hand and attempting to keep her board steady with the other. "And it looks like he just discovered your top."

"Oh, no!" Mollie wailed. "Are you sure it's my top?"

"It's either your stringy top or a handful of yellow seaweed," Cindy replied. "He's just standing there in the shallow water with your top in his hand."

"I might as well go under right here and now," Mollie declared dramatically.

"Oh, Mollie, really! You'll have to go back to shore—" Cindy stopped in midsentence as Duffy suddenly sprang into action. "Hey, what do you know! Duffy is paddling out here on his board!"

"No!"

"Yes, and he has his denim shirt tied around his neck by the sleeves. He's coming to your rescue!"

"You mean that tacky denim shirt with the pearl snaps?" The expression on Mollie's drenched face went from fearful to downright sulky.

"This is no time to be fussy about fashion," Cindy snapped.

"No, I guess you're right, Cindy." Mollie relented, resting her cheek against the board.

"Hi, girls," Duffy greeted from a few yards away.

Mollie put up a hand to stop him. "Don't come any closer! Toss me the shirt."

"Don't get shook up," Duffy said in an offended tone. "In case you haven't noticed, I'm the hero here." He loosened the knotted sleeves and tossed the shirt to Cindy's board.

"No jokes, Duffy," Cindy warned. "Mollie has suffered enough."

"I haven't said anything!" Duffy exclaimed in a wounded voice.

"Go back, please, Duffy," Mollie pleaded.

"I'm putting you back on this surfboard myself," Duffy declared with determination. "I'll cover my eyes while you put on the shirt."

"You'll peek," Mollie insisted.

"No, I won't," he growled, covering his eyes. "Hurry up, before we all end up under a tidal wave!"

Ducking under water, Mollie managed to slip into the shirt and snap it up quickly. Duffy then eased Mollie onto his surfboard and they rode back together.

The welcoming committee was waiting at the water's edge. Grant, Anna, and Carey congratulated Duffy on a job well done, with teasing remarks and slaps on the back. Mollie stood sheepishly off to the side, Duffy's soaked denim shirt hanging on her like a baggy dress. Her mascara was smudged, and her blond ponytail hung in a wet clump on the back of her head.

"You're okay, aren't you, Mollie?" Cindy asked, handing her a towel.

"I must be a total mess," Mollie complained, looking around to note several people watching her curiously. She normally liked to be the center of attention, but not at the expense of being laughed at.

"If she's worried about her looks, she must be fine," Carey pointed out.

"I can't bear for everyone to see me like this," Mollie said, dabbing her face with the towel.

"I'll take you home," Duffy offered. "We can tie your bike to the roof rack."

"Great. Thanks." Mollie stuffed her towel, lacy coverup, and skimpy top into her beach bag.

"I'll be back in a few minutes," Duffy said, jingling his keys. "Keep an eye on my stuff."

Grant emitted a low whistle as the unlikely couple walked across the sand together toward the parking lot. "Guess we've had our jolt of excitement for the day."

"I thought Duffy would've been laughing the hardest," Cindy said with a puzzled expression. "He sure is acting strange today."

"Yeah," Anna agreed, "like a human being."

Carey shook her head in wonder. "Looks like even Duffy's sense of humor has its limits."

When Cindy arrived home from the beach that afternoon, her parents were in the driveway, just about to get into the station wagon.

"Wow, are you two ever dressed up," Cindy observed, wheeling her bicycle up to the garage.

"We're going to your cousin Genie's wedding, remember?" Mrs. Lewis said, patting her carefully styled hair.

"That's right, honey," Mr. Lewis said, favoring Cindy with a wink. "Your mother is anxious to check out the catering competition."

"If John and Sherry didn't want me to cater their daughter's wedding, I am mature enough to accept it gracefully," Mrs. Lewis assured her husband crisply.

"I'm teasing, and you know it," Mr. Lewis replied, smiling as he walked around to the driver's side of the car.

"Everyone knows you're the best caterer in

Santa Barbara, Mom," Cindy said. "Uncle John and Aunt Sherry probably just wanted to give someone else a chance."

Mrs. Lewis grinned. "Now that's what I like to hear. At least I'll never have to worry about your appetite." She glanced toward the house. "Will you make sure Mollie eats something tonight? She's been up in her room ever since Duffy brought her home. Physically she's fine, but it's not like her to lock herself away."

"I'll check her out," Cindy promised.

Cindy prepared a simple meal of hamburgers and corn on the cob and brought a tray upstairs to Mollie.

"Open up," Cindy called, rapping on her sister's bedroom door.

"Come in," a muffled voice replied. "The door's unlocked."

Cindy entered the room, to find Mollie stretched out on the bed in her Garfield nightshirt, staring at the ceiling.

"You'll feel better if you eat something," Cindy said brightly, setting the tray down on a bare corner of Mollie's cosmetic-cluttered dresser.

"Thanks, Cindy," Mollie said softly.

Cindy sat down on the edge of the bed. "Mollie, do you want to talk about what happened today?"

"I suppose," Mollie said, rolling on her side to give Cindy her full attention.

"First of all, I hope you learned something while struggling out there in the water," Cindy began.

"Oh, I sure did," Mollie hastily assured her with round, intense eyes.

Cindy breathed a sigh of relief. Mollie obviously realized that she didn't belong on a surfboard any more than Nicole did. Cindy had been afraid that she'd have to give her impetuous sister a lecture on water safety.

"It was fate," Mollie said simply.

"Yes, yes, you could say that," Cindy said with a smile.

"I mean, it was meant to happen exactly the way it did. If I hadn't wiped out and lost my top, Duffy never would've come to my rescue, right?"

Cindy opened her mouth to protest, suddenly having the feeling that the conversation was taking an unexpected turn.

"I could've gone on for the next fifty years, seeing Duffy as nothing more than a carrot-topped goof. A clown who lives from prank to prank. I might never have had the chance to see him as the gentle, sensitive guy he really is deep inside."

"Oh, no," Cindy groaned. Her sister's symptoms were unmistakable.

"Oh, yes, Cindy, it is true," Mollie sighed dreamily, resting her head back on the pillow. "I'm madly in love with Duffy Duncan. And I know he's crazy about me, too."

"Mollie, Duffy is one of my dearest friends, but he hasn't transformed into a dreamy Robert Redford type all of a sudden. He has good qualities like all of us, but Duffy is ... Duffy."

"He's changed for me, Cindy," Mollie insisted firmly. "I just succeeded where you, Carey, and Anna have failed. I managed to bring out a special side to Duffy Duncan that you didn't even know existed."

"One rescue doesn't totally transform a person," Cindy maintained.

"I mean this in a nice way, Cindy, but I think it would be better if you minded your own business. I understand real romance better than you do."

Cindy stared at her sister in exasperation. Realizing that the situation was hopeless, she got to her feet and left the room.

How had Mollie managed to turn a simple good deed into a budding romance? Cindy wondered as she descended the stairs. She entered the kitchen, passed by her dinner, which was cooling on the table, and lifted the telephone receiver. It seemed only right to warn free and easy Duffy that he now had the reputation for being a gentle, sensitive hero.

Or should she warn him?

A mischievous smile suddenly lit up Cindy's face, and she set the receiver back on the hook. Maybe it would be fun to watch Duffy make that discovery himself. After all, he was the master of surprise, the guy who threw others off balance. Cindy's pal since childhood, Duffy had pulled a number of pranks on her over the years. Many incidents stuck in her mind, from the time he'd let spiders loose in her lunch box in second grade, to more recently, when he'd shown up at the Department of Motor Vehicles on the day of her road test and attached a bogus license plate to the station wagon that read TEEN SURFER—I LIVE FOR THE BEACH. She'd almost lost her chance at the test!

Cindy nodded confidently. Watching Duffy Duncan squirm under Mollie's affections could be very interesting. Most likely Mollie would flutter her lashes at him from across the lunch table for a while and call him a hero in a sultry Joan Collins voice. Then Duffy would pay her back by putting a spider in her lunch and spouting off a string of sandbox jokes. Duffy's natural behavior would definitely be enough to burst Mollie's romantic bubble and send her stomping off. Yes, Cindy decided with a satisfied nod, I'll take Mollie's advice and mind my own business.

Chapter 6

*C*indy had trouble staying awake during creative communication class on Monday morning. Even though Grant was seated directly behind her, Mr. Thomas's eagle eyes kept her from talking to him or attempting to slip him a note. Considering that Cindy and Grant thought the communications class would bring them closer together, it was sort of funny—in an annoying sort of way.

Cindy stifled a yawn as Mr. Thomas droned on about the influence newspapers had over society. She unconsciously tuned him out and gazed out the window at the traffic moving along Grove Boulevard. Grove Boulevard just happened to lead to the ocean, and as usual, Cindy's thoughts led to the same place. According to the surf reports on the radio that morning, the weather conditions were just right for riding the tubes. Cindy couldn't help but imagine all the waves rolling to shore at that very minute, with no one to ride them. It seemed like such a terrible, terrible waste....

"Miss Lewis!"

Grant's warning poke and the sharp edge of Mr. Thomas's voice jolted her back to the classroom.

"Miss Lewis, if it isn't too much trouble, I'd appreciate at least a fraction of your attention."

Cindy looked up, to find the stout, bald teacher hovering over her like a storm cloud ready to explode. "Yes, sir. You have my attention."

"Oh? If that were truly the case, you'd have last week's assignment in hand."

Cindy noted the stack of scrapbooks made of construction paper and newspaper clippings under his arm, and realized that he was collecting their homework. Cindy rummaged through the books on the corner of her desk and pulled out her collection of clippings. "Here it is."

"Thank you so much," he said briskly, adding her book to his stack.

Cindy held her breath, waiting for the most outspoken teacher in the school to move on to his next victim. He didn't budge.

"Am I boring you, Miss Lewis?" he inquired, lifting a heavy gray brow. "I've been competing with Grove Boulevard for your attention every day so far this semester and feel that I am losing by a wide margin."

"Sorry, Mr. Thomas," she murmured, aware that her face was the color and temperature of a red-hot coal.

" 'Sorry' is what we say when we bump into someone in the hallway," Mr. Thomas objected. "But it just doesn't make it in this classroom. We are supposed to be learning to communicate in here! If there is a problem, let's get it out in the open. After all, you elected to take this course instead of film study or oil painting or cooking. No one forced you to be here."

"Well, this course isn't exactly what I expected," Cindy began hesitantly.

"I thought we had a very productive first week analyzing the incredible influence the newspaper has on the public," Mr. Thomas insisted.

"I thought we'd be talking a lot," Cindy explained. "Talking to each other ..."

Mr. Thomas cast a cool, significant glance back at Grant. "I hate to disappoint you, but this is not, by any stretch of the imagination, a gossip hour for friends and steadies."

Grant's hand immediately shot up.

"Go ahead, Mr. MacPhearson," the teacher invited, "communicate with us."

"We aren't interested in gossiping during your class," Grant assured him. "We thought this class would give us tips on communicating with each other."

Jane Leonard, a perky dark-haired girl from the swim team, nodded in agreement. "Some of us thought we'd be discussing our problems, not things in the newspaper."

"Could we try talking about the stuff that happens to us?" Cindy ventured.

Mr. Thomas paused thoughtfully. "I have a solid lesson plan prepared for the entire semester." Even though his tone had a gruff edge, it was obvious that he was trying to win them over. "I have some very interesting examples of subliminal advertising in magazines and commercials. Also, I've collected some very interesting slides that send out intriguing signals to the public every day."

Groans filled the room, much to Mr. Thomas's chagrin.

"All right, Miss Lewis, I challenge you," Mr. Thomas said suddenly. "I challenge you to take on an extra-credit assignment."

Extra credit. The two simple words sent a chill down Cindy's spine. She had enough trouble staying indoors long enough to finish her regular homework. She glanced back at Grant and Duffy and found them both watching her with sympathy. "But Mr. Thomas—" Cindy began in a panic-stricken voice.

"If you come to me with a sensible lesson plan by Friday, I will let you take over the class for an entire period on Monday," he continued, ignoring her protests. "If you're successful, you will earn extra credit, and I will compromise and set aside one day a week from now on to any student who has a lucid idea."

Murmurs and cheers filled the classroom. "After all, compromise is an important part of communicating with one another," Mr. Thomas said. "Just remember that I still expect you to do all of the assignments included in my curriculum."

Everyone surrounded Cindy after class, eager to congratulate her on standing up to Mr. Thomas.

"We're counting on you, Cindy," Jane Leonard said, her brown eyes reflecting urgency.

"Tough break, kid," Duffy said, socking her arm.

"But we know you'll come through." He headed out the door before she could sock him back.

"Yeah," Doug Lucas added. "You've got to pull this off. It could mean getting a break from Mr. Dull one day a week!"

Grant slipped his arm around Cindy's shoulders and they started down the crowded hallway toward the cafeteria. "Wow, have you turned out to be a little operator," he teased. "And on an empty stomach yet!"

"This isn't funny," Cindy muttered. "I'm the last person in the world who should be dreaming up a class assignment. This is right up Nicole's alley, not mine."

"Oh, before I know it, you'll be making up lesson plans for all the teachers." Grant shook his black curly head with a heavy sigh. "No more carefree days of sun and surf. You'll bury your little blond head in all sorts of instructors' manuals and turn lily-white from lack of sunlight."

"Cut it out, MacPhearson," she threatened, making a fist, " 'cause if you don't, I'll assign the class to probe your mind with some very blunt instruments. How's that for communication?"

"Pretty darn clear, I'd say." Grant chuckled. Covering his head with his books, he ducked into the cafeteria ahead of Cindy.

They got through the lunch line as quickly as possible and joined their friends at their regular table. Duffy, who had left class only minutes ahead of them, was already polishing off his lunch.

"These chicken nuggets are the worst!" Anna complained, swallowing with a sour expression.

"Let me take them off your hands," Duffy offered, his long arm shooting across the table at Anna's plate with lightning speed.

"Hold it, Duffy!" Anna swiftly put her hand on his to stop him. "This rubber chicken is yours for one lunch ticket or some cold cash."

"Aw, forget it," Duffy said, pulling his hand away. "I thought you were going to make a donation."

"It seems like Duffy's been holding hands with all the girls lately," Grant said slyly, grinning from ear to ear.

"Huh?" Duffy stared at his best friend, his mouth hanging open in bewilderment.

Grant's blue-green eyes twinkled merrily. "Saturday it was Mollie. Today it's Anna. If I don't look out, you'll be squeezing Cindy's little fingers."

"You've got it all wrong," Duffy protested anxiously. "I wasn't trying to hold Anna's hand. I was trying to hold her chicken."

Laughter erupted around the table.

"And as far as Mollie goes," Duffy continued hotly, "she's just a kid."

"I guarantee she'll sock you if you call her one," Cindy said, munching hungrily on her nuggets and French fries. Dealing with Mr. Thomas had almost killed her appetite. Almost.

"Here she comes," Carey murmured.

Mollie was easy to spot in the crowd, dressed in her floral knit pants and satiny mint-green blouse. Her long blond hair was carefully curled and pulled away from her face with a mint-colored comb. "Hi, everybody!" she greeted the group cheerfully, setting a plastic bag down on the table beside her purse.

"Are you going to skip the lunch line again?" Cindy asked, concerned about Mollie's yo-yo eating habits.

"I have everything I need right here," Mollie replied, pulling an apple from her purse.

"What have you got in the bag?" Carey asked, "your dessert?"

"No." Mollie giggled. "It's something for Duffy."

Duffy, already red-faced from Grant's remarks, gulped under Mollie's endearing smile.

Mollie reached into the large white bag and produced Duffy's denim shirt, neatly folded and pressed.

"You didn't have to fix it up like this," Duffy said, taking the shirt from Mollie.

"She didn't," Cindy volunteered helpfully. "Our mom did."

Mollie shot her sister a ferocious glare, then turned back to Duffy with a sweet smile. "It's the thought that counts, and I watched over Mom the whole time to make sure she did a good job."

"Thanks," Duffy mumbled, stuffing the shirt down between the chairs with his books, unconcerned about keeping it neat.

"I should be thanking you for rescuing me the other day," Mollie ventured flirtatiously.

All eyes were on Duffy, eager to see what crazy stunt he would pull on Mollie. Would he make a grab for her apple? But as it turned out, Duffy didn't act like his crazy self at all.

"Just forget it, Mollie," he said in a patient tone. "It was nothing."

"But Duffy—"

Duffy scooped his things up from the floor and

jumped to his feet. "I have to stop by the chemistry lab and double-check my homework before class this afternoon. See you later."

"I'll go along," Mollie chirped. Moving as rapidly as any athlete, she collected her things and fell into step with him. "I just love chemicals and beakers and all that stuff."

"Boy, is she ever hung up on Duncan," Carey said, shaking her head in disbelief.

"Yeah," Cindy agreed between bites of chicken. "She told me so on Saturday. I never thought Duffy would let her get away with a lot of romantic gushing, though."

"Duffy isn't the romantic hero she thinks he is," Anna pointed out.

"I tried to tell her that," Cindy said, "but she told me to mind my own business."

"Duffy can handle it," Grant stated with assurance.

"I wonder if he really has a chemistry assignment to double-check," Cindy said doubtfully.

Carey laughed. "If he doesn't, he'll have to make one up!"

Chapter 7

*W*hen Cindy entered the pool area after school, she felt totally in control for the first time since the day began. She readily admitted to herself that she'd been lost and tongue-tied when confronting Mr. Thomas, and completely blown away by Mollie's exuberant behavior toward Duffy at lunch. But she was an entirely different person when faced with the physical challenges of being on the swim team. She was in peak condition mentally and physically when it came to her favorite sport.

Cindy padded across the concrete deck of the pool, tucking stray wisps of light hair under her cap, happily greeting her fellow teammates.

"Get in position for the warm-up," Coach Lawford bellowed, causing everyone to scamper to their proper lanes for their regular workout.

"Hey, Cindy!"

Cindy snapped her goggles into place and turned to face Jane Leonard in the adjoining lane.

"Way to go with old man Thomas today," she said, adjusting her own goggles on the bridge of her nose.

"Thanks."

"Have any ideas yet for your class project?" Jane asked eagerly.

Cindy shook her head. "I don't want to spoil practice by even thinking about it," she replied with determination.

"Let me know if you need some help," Jane offered. "I think we should spend the class period watching soap operas—you know, like *All My Children* and *Another World*. That's a good communication lesson, don't you think?"

"Thanks for the tip," Cindy said doubtfully. "I—"

"Lewis! Leonard!" Coach Lawford barked. "Save it for later! This is swim practice, not a tea party!" With that he blew his whistle, sending the girls springing into the water headfirst.

Cindy surfaced from her neat, shallow dive and fell into an easy rhythm of steady, even strokes. Whoever said water had a healing effect sure knew what he was talking about, she decided as she completed lap after lap in the refreshing pool.

Two hours later Cindy left the gym feeling like her old self. There was nothing like a good physical workout to loosen up tense muscles and clear the mind. Not that her problems had disappeared into thin air, she reminded herself as she walked through the nearly deserted school corridor. She still had to face Mr. Thomas's extra-credit challenge, and she still had to cope with Mollie.

Mollie . . . Cindy's steps grew heavier as she thought about her bubbly little tag-along sister. Cripes, she's really going too far. It was okay for a while. . . . I guess in a way it was even kind of fun having the shrimp along. With Nicole all the way across the country, Mollie's the only sister I have left. But why does she act so weird sometimes? Like this dumb crush on Duffy . . .

Cindy swung open Vista's double door entrance, still deep in thought. She was so distracted that she didn't notice Heather standing on the steps in her path and plowed right into her.

"Oops!" Cindy exclaimed, stepping back to steady herself. "Sorry, Heather."

"That's okay," Heather said breathlessly. She struggled to balance a grocery bag in one hand, reaching for the iron rail with the other.

"There's hardly ever anyone lingering on the steps at this time of day," Cindy said in an apologetic tone. "But I should've been more careful anyway."

"I've been waiting for you," Heather said.

"Why?" Cindy asked in a mixture of surprise and hope. It had to be about Mollie.

"This is for you—for Mollie, I mean," Heather stammered, thrusting the bulky brown bag into Cindy's arms.

"What is it?" Cindy asked, peeking inside the bag. A peace offering, maybe? A quick inventory revealed a curling iron, an algebra book, a few bottles of nail polish, a romance novel, and several other odds and ends.

"I wondered where my fuzzy yellow slippers got to," Cindy murmured.

Heather blushed a little. "Mollie wore those at my last sleep-over because they matched the quilted yellow robe she borrowed from your mother. And she stained the left toe herself," Heather added defensively. "We were drinking Diet Cokes during a *Midnight Monster Mania* movie, and she jiggled her can during a real scary part."

"Sounds like a fun party," Cindy ventured. "Of course you guys always have a lot of fun together. I guess you all have a lot in common."

Heather's grim expression didn't waver. "Linda, Sarah, and I still have a lot in common. We haven't changed."

"You can't just drop Mollie," Cindy blurted out in protest.

"She dropped us," Heather snapped, her eyes glistening. "We can't measure up to a crowd of juniors." She turned on her heel and scurried down the last several steps.

"Heather! Please wait!"

"Tell Mollie we want our stuff back, too," Heather called over her shoulder.

"How am I supposed to handle Mollie?" Cindy shouted after the retreating figure. "How am I supposed to handle this bag while riding my bike?" she grumbled, frowning down at the bicycle rack beside the concrete stairs.

"What took you so long, Cindy?" Mollie called from the front steps of the Lewis house. "Mom has some kind of awesome surprise for us!"

Cindy flashed Mollie an annoyed look and continued to pump her bicycle up the driveway toward the garage.

"Why are you lugging that old brown bag around?" Mollie asked as she followed Cindy into the garage. "Did you lose your nylon tote?"

"No, I didn't lose my tote," Cindy shot back, parking her bike near the station wagon. "I had to leave my swimming gear at school so I could lug this stuff home to you!" She tossed Mollie the bag.

"Hah!" Mollie dug into the bag with a gasp. "Those dirty rats! Those—those children," she sputtered, her round blue eyes full of hurt and anger.

"If you've been ignoring them, they have a right to be angry," Cindy pointed out, her tone softening.

"I don't ignore them, not all the time," Mollie insisted. "I've just been really busy lately. Besides, I just don't fit in with them anymore. They should try to be more understanding."

"Why don't you give them another chance? I think they're hurt that you've cut them off," Cindy said, giving Mollie's shoulders a squeeze.

"They're just jealous that I've moved up in the world," Mollie claimed with her own unique logic.

"Oh, Mollie . . ." Cindy sighed with resignation.

"I don't want to talk about them anymore!" Mollie cried, flying through the connecting door to the house.

Cindy followed at a slower pace, stopping in the kitchen to greet her mother.

"What was in that bag you gave Mollie?" Laura Lewis asked, dropping peeled potatoes into a kettle on the stove. "Rattlesnakes?"

"Sort of," Cindy replied, opening the refrigerator. "Why is the mother always the last to know when trouble is brewing?" Mrs. Lewis asked, turning on the burner under the kettle.

"Trouble moves in pretty fast sometimes," Cindy said, pulling an apple out of the crisper. "I'm starving. What's for dinner, besides potatoes, that is?"

"Meat loaf. Now, tell me what's going on with Mollie," Mrs. Lewis prodded, steering Cindy over to the kitchen table.

Cindy sat down with her mother and bit into her apple. "Heather, Linda, and Sarah have taken a major step in the feud. They've returned all of Mollie's things—and a few of our things, too," Cindy added, thinking of her fuzzy slippers and her mother's steamy historical paperback.

"Oh, dear," Laura Lewis lamented, her blue eyes full of concern. "I never thought their separation would progress this far."

"I never thought her fascination with my friends would progress this far," Cindy added.

"Do you know, she stood over me the entire time I washed and ironed Duffy's shirt?" A trace of annoyance crossed Mrs. Lewis's face.

Cindy nodded with a grin. "Mollie can appreciate quality work when she sees it."

"Well, this certainly has spoiled my surprise," Mrs. Lewis said with disappointment.

"Mollie mentioned that you had something to tell us," Cindy said, brimming with curiosity.

Suddenly a hiss of water interrupted them. "My potatoes!" Mrs. Lewis rushed over to the pot boiling over on the stove.

"Don't leave me in suspense," Cindy pleaded.

"We'll talk at dinner," her mother promised, turning down the burner and grabbing a hot pad.

"Meat loaf!" Mr. Lewis enthused an hour later, rubbing his hands together in anticipation. He took a thick slice of meat from the platter and passed it on to Mollie. "Be sure you take some, Mollie. Have some mashed potatoes, too."

"You're priceless, Richard," Laura Lewis scoffed good-naturedly. "I treat this family to every delicacy ever made at Moveable Feasts, and you go bonkers over a pound of hamburger mixed with cracker crumbs and tomato sauce!"

"Don't forget the onions," her husband said with an appreciative sniff.

"So, Mom, tell us about the surprise," Cindy prompted, digging into her food with gusto.

"Remember the business luncheon I catered for Beth Dougherty, the concert promoter?"

Cindy nodded vigorously. Even Mollie, who was picking at her food with her fork, perked up all of a sudden.

"Beth was so grateful for the last-minute details I ironed out that she sent me six tickets to the Cyndi Lauper concert on Saturday."

Mollie lit up like a beacon. "That is totally awesome! Wow! Mom, that's fantastic!"

"Yeah, Mom. Thanks!" Cindy exclaimed. She paused, glancing at her parents with a twinkle in her eye. "Don't you and Dad want to bring some of your friends to the concert?"

Mr. Lewis nearly choked on his mashed potatoes as he let out a hearty laugh. "I think I'll wait until John Denver comes around. He's more my speed, don't you agree?"

Cindy opened her mouth to reply, when Mollie interrupted. "Don't you think I look kind of like Cyndi Lauper?" she asked. "I mean, if I dyed my hair red."

"I can hardly tell the two of you apart," Cindy said, rolling her eyes.

"I can already picture it," Mr. Lewis said, shaking his head. "Cindy and Grant will shoot off in that fancy red Trans Am of his, and I'll be driving Mollie to the concert with a bunch of giggly girls in the back of the station wagon."

Mollie cast a pained look in her father's direction. "There are exactly enough tickets for me, Cindy, Duffy, Grant, Anne, and Carey," she said, ticking a finger with every name.

Mr. Lewis was taken aback. "What's going on? I feel like I've just walked in on the middle of a movie—a psychological thriller where the family tries to drive the father crazy." He looked from his daughters to his wife.

"More like a screwball comedy, Dad," Cindy explained. "Mollie has traded her friends for mine."

Mr. Lewis exchanged a skeptical look with his wife, but said nothing.

"I can't wait until Saturday night!" Mollie exclaimed, her round blue eyes glowing. "I'll have to start preparing tonight."

"Today is only Monday," her mother reminded her.

"I know, but I'll have to give myself a manicure, for starters," Mollie replied, pushing back her chair.

"What about your dinner, dear?" Mrs. Lewis protested.

"I'm finished." Mollie said, impulsively grabbing a roll from the basket on the table. "Saturday might be the most important night of my life!"

"Mollie certainly expects a lot from a concert," Mr. Lewis said, taking a roll for himself.

Mollie certainly expects a lot from Duffy, Cindy amended silently. She knew exactly what her sister was thinking. Where will it all end? she wondered.

Cindy joined the crowd at the school hangout, Pete's Pizzeria, Tuesday afternoon after swim practice. They were all jammed into a booth, munching on a large sausage pizza.

"It's about time," Duffy complained, biting into a slice of crust smothered with toppings. Tomato sauce, the same shade as his hair, dotted his chin. "Mollie's having a heck of a time keeping the Lewis family secret. She's just about to burst wide open."

"How was practice?" Grant asked. He stood up to give Cindy his place and pulled a chair from an adjoining table for himself.

"Great," Cindy said brightly.

"The secret, Cindy, the secret," Carey prodded over the rim of her glass.

Cindy smiled with amusement. She had made Mollie promise to keep her mouth shut so she could break the good news to her friends herself. "We all have front row seats to the Cyndi Lauper concert next Saturday night!"

As whoops of surprise and delight filled the booth, Cindy passed out the tickets.

"I'll guard this ticket with my life," Grant said, slipping it into his wallet.

"I'm putting mine in a safe place, too," Anna said, dropping it into her denim purse.

"How will you ever find it again in that sack of junk?" Duffy demanded.

"You're talking to someone who's seen the inside of your locker," Anna fired back with a wicked grin. "Talk about junk! You've got a huge bag of confetti from last year's homecoming game stuffed in the back corner, as well as some high-top sneakers you wore for basketball in the eighth grade. And, you have a yellowed poster of Charlie's Angels hanging on the inside of the door."

"Snoop!" Duffy accused.

"Don't be so hard on Duffy," Mollie scolded.

"I don't need protection, Mol," Duffy cut in, softening his words with a lopsided smile. "These girls wouldn't bother to get out of bed in the morning if they didn't have me to harrass."

Cindy, Carey, and Anna moaned in unison.

"You poor baby," Cindy clucked sweetly, ruffling Duffy's red hair.

"Good old Duffy," Anna said, tweaking his cheek.

Carey nodded in agreement. "Torturing Duffy gives me a good reason to come to school every day. He'd be lost without an insult or two every hour."

Mollie frowned at the girls in frustration. How could they be so rough on Duffy when he was so sweet? Well, she figured smugly, when Duffy and I start going steady, all of the horseplay will stop. They'll treat him with respect, or else! No more of this face tweaking and hair ruffling!

"We'll have to arrange transportation," Grant was saying. "Cindy and I can easily take Mollie along in the Trans Am."

"I'll pick up Carey and Anna," Duffy offered.

"Hey, why can't I ride with Duffy?" Mollie protested.

"Because Grant is coming to our house anyway," Cindy pointed out sensibly.

If only Duffy would come right out and ask me for a date, Mollie groaned inwardly. But he'll never muster up the courage, with all the others teasing him all the time. Somehow I've just got to get a seat beside Duffy at the concert, she decided.

Cindy glanced over at Mollie, who was staring dreamily into space. She knew what her little sister was thinking. Mollie wanted to date Duffy in the worst way. Well, Cindy vowed silently, if it was the last thing she did, she was going to keep them apart at the concert!

Chapter 8

"*C*indy, what are you doing out in the back-yard at this time of night?" Mollie asked, surprised to find her sister pacing across the Lewises' brick patio under the moonlight. "It's a few minutes past nine."

Cindy paused and shoved her hands into the pockets of her faded blue jeans. "Oh, Mollie," she said absentmindedly, "I didn't realize it was that late."

When Cindy began to pace again rather than come inside, Mollie stepped through the sliding glass door to join her. "Kind of nice out here," she said, looking up at the blue star-studded sky.

Cindy looked up at the sky as if seeing it for the first time. "Yeah, guess it is."

Mollie sat down on the wooden swing near the barbecue and tucked her feet under her legs. The swing creaked in protest as she began to rock slowly. "So, Cindy, what's the big problem that's got you all wound up?"

Cindy turned toward her with a troubled frown. "Is it that obvious?"

"It sure is," Mollie replied without hesitation. "It takes a lot to get you uptight. You're our family optimist, remember?"

"The family optimist is sinking fast this time," Cindy lamented, throwing her hands into the air. "It's Thursday, and I still don't know what to do for my creative communication project! If I don't come up with a super idea by class tomorrow morning, Mr. Thomas will pulverize me!"

"Can't you just tell him that you bombed?" Mollie suggested, twirling a golden lock thoughtfully around her finger. "I mean, he just dumped this extra-credit mess on you."

"A Lewis never gives up!" Cindy declared. "I got myself into this jam by daydreaming during class, and now I have to bail myself out!"

"Don't be so hard on yourself," Mollie comforted. "It's not your fault that Mr. Thomas is dull."

"I'd like nothing better than to come up with a super idea, but so far I've come up with a big round zero."

"Maybe you're blocking out your thought waves by simply trying too hard," Mollie suggested. "It's never happened to me personally, but I heard something on Stan Sting's radio show a few weeks ago about how to overcome a mental block."

Cindy shook her head and rubbed her temples. "I think you've hit it on the nose, shrimp," she said wearily. "The entire class is counting on me. And they won't let me forget it for a minute."

"Too bad Nicole isn't here," Mollie remarked. "We could always count on her to solve the real brainteasers."

"It was nice to turn to her in a pinch," Cindy agreed.

"Hey, why don't you call her?" Mollie suggested with sudden inspiration.

"I could. . . ." Cindy's voice trailed off as she considered the idea. On the one hand, she hated to burden Nicole with her problems, considering how down Nicole was when she called last week. But misery loves company, doesn't it? she reminded herself. Maybe it will even make Nicole feel better if she has a dilemma from home to ponder over for a while.

"Sure, you could call," Mollie coaxed, excited over the prospect of contacting their older sister. "We can both talk to her!"

"Let's go for it!" Cindy decided brightly, marching across the patio with new confidence in her step and Mollie close behind.

Cindy picked up the phone in the kitchen and anxiously punched in the number from the message board. "It's ringing," she said, leaning against the wall.

"Well?" Mollie demanded, her hands planted on her hips.

"It's still ringing, Mollie," Cindy reported with disappointment. Just as she was about to hang up, Cindy heard a click and a heavy sigh on the line.

"Hel—hello?"

"Nicole? Is that you?"

"*Oui*, it's me," Nicole mumbled.

"You sound strange," Cindy commented, casting Mollie a worried frown.

Nicole cleared her throat. "Do you know what time it is?"

Cindy glanced at the clock. "Sure. It's nine-fifteen."

"It's nine-fifteen in Santa Barbara," Nicole said groggily, "but it's twelve-fifteen in Boston."

"Oh, no! I suppose you were sound asleep," Cindy murmured contritely.

"Of course I was. It's a school night, and I've got an early class tomorrow."

"What's wrong?" Mollie demanded, tugging at the sleeve of Cindy's short-sleeved plaid blouse.

"We forgot about the time difference, Mollie," Cindy hastened to explain.

"Cindy, is there a family emergency?" Nicole asked nervously.

"No, there's no family emergency. I just have a private crisis I want to talk over with you."

"Now?"

"I'm sort of on a time limit," Cindy admitted hesitantly.

"Qu'est-ce qui ne marche pas?" Nicole gave in.

Cindy told her about the extra-credit assignment.

"You'll think more clearly if you remain calm," Nicole advised, not bothering to stifle a huge yawn. "Now, exactly what did you want from the class in the first place?"

"I wanted the chance to talk. There should be more to communication than listening, right?"

"Oui. Let's take this step-by-step," Nicole proposed thoughtfully. "Perhaps your project should center around giving everyone the opportunity to say something."

"Good start," Cindy agreed, already gaining confidence.

"What does communication mean to you? Now think, Cindy. Tell me the first thing that pops into your mind."

"Truth," Cindy said immediately.

"Good answer," Nicole praised groggily. "Take it a step further. What could you do with those ideas in a classroom?"

Cindy paused to think.

"Don't forget this is a long-distance call," Mollie broke in impatiently.

"How about an honesty hour?" Cindy said with sudden inspiration. "All the kids would have a chance to talk, on the condition that they promised to be completely open and tell the truth."

"Mon Dieu!" Nicole gasped in horror. "You might start a riot."

"Maybe," Cindy said, "but no one would dare accuse me of being dull."

Nicole yawned again as if on cue.

"Thanks a lot, Nicole, you really saved my neck. Sorry I woke you," Cindy said. "So how are things going for you?" she added with concern.

"Magnifiquement!" she murmured sleepily. "I've made two good friends who appreciate me just as I am."

"That's super! What are they like?"

"A brother and sister—Kent and JoAnne Fortney."

"Sounds like your social life has taken off," Cindy noted happily, pushing Mollie's persistent hand away from the phone.

"I haven't even told the best part yet. Kent and JoAnne have actually visited Paris!"

"Wow! No wonder you hit it off so well."

"Oh, Cindy, they saw everything, from the Cathedral of Nôtre-Dame to the Sacré-Coeur."

"Isn't the Sacré-Coeur the church with that heavy bell?" Cindy asked.

"*Oui*. It weighs nearly nineteen tons. And they've been to the top of the Eiffel Tower." She sighed softly. "I could go on forever about the wonderful stories they told me."

"That's great, Nicole," Cindy replied.

"And, Cindy, Kent looks just like Matt Dillon," Nicole confided. "Oh, *mon Dieu*! I sound like Mollie, don't I?"

"*Oh, là là!*" Cindy giggled.

"I suppose Mollie is waiting to talk to me," Nicole said wearily.

"Yeah, but let me tell you about her surfing adventure first."

"Mollie actually went surfing?" Nicole questioned in surprise.

"For a minute or two anyway." Cindy went on to describe Mollie's unfortunate choice in surfing swimwear and Duffy's daring rescue.

Mollie finally could stand it no longer and wrenched the phone from Cindy's grip. "Nicole? Nicole?" she said anxiously. "She isn't answering, Cindy," Mollie said, puzzled. She listened intently for a moment, then scowled. "It sounds like she's snoring. . . . You actually put her to sleep!" Mollie slammed the receiver back in place. "Thanks loads, Cindy! You bored her unconscious!"

"Your surfing escapade put her to sleep," Cindy argued.

"What a total waste of time!"

"It was not," Cindy said, folding her tanned

arms across her chest. "With Nicole's help, I've managed to come up with an extra-credit project."

Cindy outlined her idea for an honesty hour on a sheet of paper and gave it to Mr. Thomas at the beginning of class on Friday morning.

He stood over her desk for what seemed like a lifetime, examining her plan. Her outline had made the rounds before the bell rang, so most of the students already knew about her idea and were waiting anxiously along with Cindy.

"I heartily approve of your suggestion, Miss Lewis," he said at last, his gruff tone holding a twinge of admiration. "You are correct in proposing that communication should be based on truth. And no age group seems to have more trouble expressing their real feelings than teenagers." He nodded his bald head eagerly. "Yes, I think this would be a wonderful experiment."

The class began to murmur with excitement.

"And to make this a more fulfilling project, I am going to ask each of you to write a report on what you learn during our honesty hour."

Groans filled the room, but Cindy was so relieved Mr. Thomas had accepted her proposal, that for once she didn't care about the report.

"Now, shall we return to today's lecture on the awesome power of the press?" he asked, his bushy gray brows narrowing threateningly.

"No!" they exclaimed unanimously.

Cindy grinned. She was sure Mr. Thomas hadn't expected such a rousing display of creative communication.

Chapter 9

*W*hen Mollie offered to give Cindy and her friends a facial on Saturday in preparation for the Cyndi Lauper concert, Cindy balked.

"Sorry, shrimp," she told her sister. "Not interested."

"But don't you all want to look your best for the concert?" Mollie asked.

Carey grinned. "We already do, Mol, We don't have to put any gunk on our faces to look our best."

"That's where you're wrong, Carey. A facial can help you look even better," Mollie declared. "How about it, gang?"

"No," Cindy said, then realized her voice had sounded a little too sharp. "We appreciate the offer, but I think the natural look is more our style. Right, girls?" she added, looking at her friends.

Anna shrugged. "It can't hurt to try it."

Mollie's face lit up. "That's the spirit! She held up a jar of amber gel. "This is Apricot Surrender, the finest facial treatment that money can buy. I baby-sat the Johnson twins an entire afternoon to pay for it."

"Oh, all right. I'll do it," Cindy grumbled.

"Count me in, then," Carey said. "What have I got to lose?"

"Good. You'll thank me when I'm done. It's the very best the beauty supply house has to offer," Mollie continued, enjoying her role as beauty consultant. "It says right here on the jar that Cybill Shepherd swears by it."

"Is that the same stuff you were using last week?" Cindy asked. "It didn't do much for your face, but it sure smelled good," she teased.

"Ha-ha," Mollie retorted good-naturedly. "That was Heather's lemon-chiffon face cream. She left a quarter of a jar here from one of our last make-over sleep-overs." A forlorn look crossed her features for a moment; then the enthusiastic smile reappeared. "But I'm sure this stuff is much, much better."

"Let's get this treatment started," Cindy said, glancing at her watch. "We'd better hurry so Carey and Anna will have plenty of time to go home and get changed."

Mollie threw a towel over her shoulder and set a folding chair up in front of the full-length mirror on Cindy's wall. "I'm ready for my first customer," she announced. The fragrance of apricots filled the room as Mollie stirred the gel with a small plastic spoon.

"Go ahead, Cindy," Carey invited.

Cindy rose from the floor in one fluid motion and slipped into the chair. "Okay, Mollie, do your stuff," she said. She stared at her reflection in the mirror. Maybe my face is kind of dull, she thought. My tan is beginning to look more like dirt.

Mollie efficiently tucked Cindy's short blond hair into a shower cap and began to rub the gel on her sister's face in a massaging, circular motion. "Just relax your facial muscles," she instructed in a professional tone. "Let the natural essence of the apricot open and refresh your pores."

Before long, all three girls were walking around the room with shower caps on their heads and a layer of amber-colored gel on their faces.

"How long do we have to wear this stuff?" Carey asked, trying to talk without upsetting the rubbery mask.

"The label on the jar is a little scuffed, but the lemon-chiffon cream instructions had an hour time limit."

"That seems like a long time," Anna remarked, sitting down on the edge of Cindy's bed.

"Yes, it does," Cindy agreed. "And this stuff is beginning to sting."

"Facials tingle," Mollie corrected. "Dog bites and paper cuts sting."

"This stings," Carey insisted.

"The path to true beauty can be a little painful sometimes," Mollie said airily, setting her mother's egg timer for sixty minutes. "By five-thirty you'll have cheeks as smooth as a baby's."

Three orange faces glared back at Mollie.

"Just sit there," Mollie ordered, trying to hide her uncertainty with a gruff voice. The lemon facial wasn't a bit painful, she recalled. I guess the apricot formula must have some special ingredient. She glanced over at the others and couldn't help grinning.

"What's so funny?" Cindy demanded, crossing her arms across her chest.

"You girls look sort of silly with orange faces," Mollie claimed with a laugh. "I'm going downstairs for a while. I feel like cracking up whenever I look at you."

"Hey," Cindy yelled after her, "now you know how the family feels whenever you wear one of these masks down to dinner!"

By the time the girls heard the ping of the timer on an hour, it had already seemed more like two and a half, but Mollie still hadn't returned.

"Let's get this stuff off," Cindy said, tossing her surfer magazine aside. The three girls rushed over to the full-length mirror.

"Does your face hurt as much as mine does?" Anne asked.

"Yes!" Cindy and Carey assured her in unison.

"These masks are supposed to peel right off, aren't they?" Carey asked.

"That's the way Mollie does it," Cindy agreed pulling at the edge of the mask under her chin. "Ouch!" she cried, dropping her hand away from her face.

"Maybe it would be easier to loosen from the top," Anna suggested, slipping her fingernail under the gel at her hairline. "Ooh! Don't try it!"

"Something's gone wrong," Cindy said in alarm. She swung open the bedroom door and shouted at the top of her lungs. "Mollie Lewis! Get up here on the double!"

Mollie raced into the room with Laura Lewis at her heels. "What's the matter?" Mollie asked, her round blue eyes full of innocence.

"Everything!" Cindy cried. "We can't get this stuff off."

"Nonsense," Mrs. Lewis said calmly, touching Cindy's cheek.

"Ouch!" Cindy said, flinching out of her mother's reach. "This gook is poison!"

Anna picked up the empty facial jar and began to examine it.

"But if Cybill Shepherd stands by this—" Mollie began.

"For your information, Mollie," Anna cut in, "Cybill Shepherd does not spell her name S-y-b-i-l."

"Everybody on earth knows that!" Cindy exploded in fury, her hands balled into fists.

Mrs. Lewis took the jar from Anna. "Mollie, how many times have I warned you about buying cheap off-brand cosmetics? According to the date on this jar, this gel expired months ago."

"Cheap?" Cindy snapped. "Off-brand? Mollie said she spent all her baby-sitting money on it."

Mollie cringed under their interrogating eyes. "I did spend all my baby-sitting money on it," she insisted. "You remember—when I took the Johnson twins trick-or-treating on Halloween."

"Trick or treating!" Cindy echoed. "But that must have been nearly a year ago."

"Well maybe it was," Mollie admitted sheepishly. "I forgot about it until this morning when I found the jar in the back of my dresser drawer.

But I didn't mean any harm. I thought it would work fine, honest!"

"We're desperate, Mrs. Lewis," Carey pleaded, her eyes watering. "Please help us!"

"I'm going to call Mrs. Borden down the street. She's a retired nurse, and I'm certain she worked in a dermatologist's office for quite some time." Mrs. Lewis headed for the telephone stand in the hallway.

"We should be dressing for the concert right now," Carey said mournfully, glancing at the alarm clock on the dresser.

"Do you think you guys will still be able to make it?" Mollie asked, casting a doubtful glance at Cindy.

"What do you think?" Cindy replied in a soft, menacing voice. She moved slowly toward her sister, raising her hands to the level of Mollie's throat.

"You aren't thinking of choking me, are you?" Mollie gulped nervously.

"You won't feel a thing," Cindy promised through clenched teeth. "Just relax your facial muscles...."

Mrs. Lewis reappeared just in time to act as peacemaker, and she moved between her daughters. "Mrs. Borden will be over in a few minutes. She suggested that we apply soothing cool towels to your faces in the meantime."

"Oh, you guys, I'm so sorry," Mollie said sincerely. "It doesn't look like you will be able to go to the concert, and it's all my fault." She sighed heavily. "I know. Why don't I call Duffy?" she asked, perking up at the idea. "He may as well ride with me and Grant, now that you'll all be out of commission." As Mollie flew through the doorway, Cindy shook her fist at her sister.

Mrs. Lewis patted Cindy comfortingly on the back. "No matter how circumstantial the evidence, honey, you must know that Mollie didn't do this on purpose."

Anna and Carey turned to Cindy for her opinion. Cindy nodded reluctantly. "Mollie's only guilty of being dumb. She doesn't have a diabolical bone in her body."

"Diabolical or dumb doesn't change the fact that we're going to miss that concert," Anna complained.

"You're right," Cindy agreed. "Nothing is going to change that."

Mrs. Borden, a plump, gray-haired woman in her sixties, arrived minutes later and took charge of the facial crisis with clucking concern. She took the girls into the bathroom one by one in the order Mollie had given them the facials, and started the careful process of dissolving their masks with cool water and a soft sponge.

"All off, Cindy," Mrs. Borden said after what seemed like an eternity. She handed her a tube of ointment. "Spread this aloe on your face, dear, and send in patient number two."

Cindy returned to her bedroom, to find Anna and Carey standing at the window overlooking the front yard. "Your turn, Carey."

Anna pulled Cindy closer to the window. "Grant is here already."

"What?" Cindy gasped, staring down at the driveway through the pane of glass. Sure enough, there was Grant's red Trans Am. And there was Mollie, dressed head to toe in washed-out denim with pink accessories, climbing into the passenger seat.

"You should go talk to him," Anna told her with a troubled frown.

"Why doesn't he come inside?" Cindy wondered aloud. "Look, he's not even getting out of the car. Doesn't he care that I nearly had my face peeled off? Oh, I'm so mad!" Cindy stamped her foot in helpless anger. "Grant is going off to that concert without even a second thought for me."

"At least, if he had stopped to talk, you could've told him to try and keep Mollie and Duffy apart," Anna added.

With a sinking feeling in her stomach, Cindy watched the Trans Am disappear down the street. Then she reluctantly moved over to the mirror to apply the ointment on her irritated skin. "Has Duffy told you how he feels about Mollie's crush?"

"He's uncomfortable," Anna replied. "Maybe for the first time in his life!"

"I thought it would be kind of funny to watch him squirm in Mollie's romantic clutches, but now I'm sorry I didn't warn him."

"What good would that have done?" Anna asked. "You tried to stop Mollie, and she told you to mind your own business."

"Guess you're right," Cindy agreed with a sigh.

Cindy went to bed that night around eleven and found that she couldn't sleep. She tossed and turned constantly, punching her pillow with every roll. Everything was a mess. Mrs. Borden had banned her from the beach for a few days and warned against even going to swim practice.

And Mollie was still out with the guys.

It was close to midnight when Cindy finally heard the rumble of the Trans Am in the driveway. Mollie bounced up the stairs in her pink heels a short time later.

"Cindy, it happened!" she squealed, bouncing on the edge of her sister's bed.

Cindy sat up like a tightly coiled spring. "What do you mean, Mollie?"

"Duffy and I kissed! It was like firecrackers. No—no," she babbled, waving her hands. "It was like dynamite! We had a perfect evening. Duffy's a dream date."

"Where was Grant during this dream date?" Cindy demanded sharply.

"Around. I didn't pay much attention to him. He was kind of a dud. Are you sure he's as cool as you say?"

"Maybe he seemed like a dud because he didn't have anyone to talk to," Cindy pointed out defensively, even though her anger toward him and the whole situation was simmering on the edge of full boil.

"Maybe." Mollie shrugged. "You really missed a great concert, Cin. Cyndi Lauper was charged up to the max. And we were so close, I could almost reach out and touch her skirt!"

"Great."

"You know, Cindy, you must be growing up," Mollie observed sagely. "It was really mature of you to let Grant tag along with us while you were stuck here with a sore face."

"I really didn't have a choice, did I?" Cindy

muttered. "He took off before I even had a chance to talk to him."

"Are you mad about something?" Mollie asked in surprise.

"I'm mad about everything!" Cindy snapped. "I'm mad at you for buying that crummy facial gel. I'm mad at Grant for going without me tonight. I'm mad about—about a lot of things!"

"Gee," Mollie said breathlessly, sliding off the bed. "I'll leave you alone. No reason for both of us to get bummed out."

Cindy punched her pillow. "No reason at all!"

Cindy awoke early on Sunday morning despite her restless night. She hopped out of bed eager to begin her routine jog along the beach. But just as she was pulling on her peach-colored sweatpants she remembered Mrs. Borden's order to stay clear of the ocean. Cindy continued to dress anyway, deciding that a jog around the neighborhood would be better than nothing. And she had Winston to think about. The family's playful Newfoundland dog would be waiting for her out in the garage. No doubt he would miss poking around in the sand and seaweed, too. But it just couldn't be helped.

Cindy set all her cares aside as she and Winston trotted up and down the neighboring tree-lined streets. It was funny how much more you noticed when you were on foot rather than on wheels, Cindy thought with amazement. The Simmons family two blocks over were putting in a swimming pool in the backyard, and old Mrs. Withers was in desperate need of some new lawn furniture. But the most interesting discovery of all was coming upon Heather out in her driveway washing her dad's Mustang.

"Hi, Heather!" Cindy waved cheerily from the street.

Heather shot her a curious glance, then continued to rub her foamy sponge along the back fender of the car.

Feeling that she had Heather nicely cornered for a chat, Cindy ran up the driveway.

"What happened to your face?" Heather asked. "Did you stay out in the sun too long?"

"I got a hold of some deadly facial gel," Cindy explained.

"You should've gone to Mollie for advice before you bought just any old thing," Heather said, shaking her head in sympathy. "She's an expert."

"I'll remember that," Cindy said, dismissing the subject. "Yeah, about Mollie—"

"I don't want to talk about that traitor," Heather interrupted, dipping her sponge in the bucket.

"You brought her up," Cindy protested.

"Only for a minute," Heather argued.

"So, how are Linda and Sarah?"

"Fine." Heather moved to the side of the Mustang and slipped the wet sponge on the roof with a plop. "You know, Mollie's really missing out on a lot of fun stuff. We're going over to the mall this afternoon to check out the huge sales. You know, I bet you'd be able to pick up a good facial cream at the beauty shop."

"Thanks for the advice," Cindy said, stroking Winston's fluffy black coat. "But I'm finished with beauty treatments."

"Nice of you to stop by," Heather said, picking up the garden hose.

"Yeah. See ya." Cindy jogged back down the driveway, relieved that Heather was angry enough at Mollie to still care.

Cindy started for home, wondering if there was any way to reunite Mollie with her friends. She belonged with them, no doubt about it. Why, oh, why did Duffy kiss Mollie? she wondered with irritation. She was as disgusted with him as she was with Grant. Duffy hadn't encouraged Mollie one bit until last night. It was a stupid thing to do if he didn't want to date her.

Cindy was more disgusted with herself than anyone else, she suddenly realized. No matter how her friends treated Mollie, Cindy felt the whole dilemma was mainly her fault. She was the one who had allowed Mollie to hang out with them, but she realized now that it wouldn't make up for missing Nicole. The three Lewis sisters had always been close but had managed to lead separate lives just the same. There wouldn't be any peace in Cindy's life until things were set right again.

Chapter 10

*C*indy walked into creative communication class on Monday morning, to find the desks arranged in a wide circle around the room.

"Choose any seat, students," Mr. Thomas announced briskly. "We'll be dispensing with our regular seating arrangement for today's discussion."

"Come sit with me, Cindy," Jane Leonard invited from the back of the room near the bookcases.

Cindy noticed Grant and Duffy out of the corner of her eye, seated together across the room near the windows, and gratefully accepted Jane's invitation. Both of the boys had called her a couple of times on Sunday and she'd stubbornly refused to talk to either one of them.

The bell rang and Mr. Thomas entered the center of the circle. "Welcome to our honesty hour, ladies and gentlemen. You are seated in a circle today so that you can face the person who is speaking at any given moment. I will retire to my desk now and let Miss Lewis take over the class."

Cindy's heart jolted as all eyes turned in her direction. "Does anyone have a special topic they'd like to talk about?" she asked, clearing her throat nervously.

To her relief Nick Webster's hand shot up. "Yes, Nick?" she said.

"I don't think there should be such strict rules in study hall," he protested. "It's tough to be quiet during the entire hour."

"It is tough," Sue Stern agreed, "but it would be impossible to concentrate on homework if everyone was making noise."

"There are times when I would like to ask someone about an assignment," Nick said. "The rule about being quiet stops me from getting help when I need it."

"It would turn into a three-ring circus," Doug Kisner added. "Monitors can't run up to everyone who is talking and ask them if they're discussing schoolwork."

"It's too bad something can't be worked out," Jane Leonard put in. "A sophomore was in a real jam last week with an algebra problem, and I felt it was only right to help her out. . . ."

Cindy tapped her pencil on her notebook and glanced over at Grant, to find him already gazing at her. As they made eye contact, Cindy's heart leaped into a double time beat and a warm blush crept up her face. Grant's blue-green eyes were full of confusion, and one black brow was lifted in question, as if asking what was going on.

As if he doesn't know! Cindy thought, shifting

restlessly in her seat. How could he take off for that concert without even checking on me? The misery she had felt sitting alone on Saturday night was still bubbling within her memory, keeping the hurt and anger fresh. With determination Cindy turned her attention back to Jane and the class, where it belonged. It was a wise thing to do, for the discussion on talking during study hall was winding down.

"I'm going to write a letter to the principal about this," Jane was saying.

"I'll help you," Nick volunteered.

"Does anyone else have a topic they'd like to talk about?" Cindy asked.

Rebecca Fowler raised her hand hesitantly. "I was wondering ..." she began, pushing her glasses up on her nose. "Does anyone else have an early curfew over the weekend? I hardly ever have time to stop at Pete's Pizzeria after the movie on Saturday night. I always have to rush right home."

Three hands immediately popped into the air and a lively debate began.

Much to Cindy's relief the class went smoothly right up until the dismissal bell rang. Topics up for discussion varied from sibling rivalry to earning an allowance.

Cindy was worried about facing Grant after class, but he left in a cluster of students, not looking back.

"Hey, sport," Duffy said, ruffling Cindy's short, flyaway curls. "Looks like Vista has a junior Barbara Walters in the making."

Cindy glared at Duffy. Well, she certainly had a long list of questions to ask him! Number one, what was he trying to prove by kissing Mollie? But as Cindy opened her mouth to begin, Mr. Thomas joined them. "Congratulations, Miss Lewis. Your honesty hour was a smashing success. I intend to mark down your extra-credit points in my grade book right now." He turned to Duffy with a broad smile. "Since you are so amused by Cindy's performance today, young man, I will put you in charge of next Monday's class. Who knows? Perhaps we'll discover that Vista has a junior Dan Rather in the making." He turned on his heel and headed for his desk, leaving Duffy behind in shock.

"Gross break," Duffy muttered.

"I'd like to tell you it's painless, but I can't," Cindy said, collecting her book.

"Why didn't you come to the phone yesterday when I called?" Duffy demanded incredulously.

Cindy glared at him. "Because I was so mad yesterday that I knew I couldn't discuss things without blowing up."

"Don't blame Grant and me if you got stuck with a bummer beauty cream," Duffy flared.

"I think there's a little more to it than that," Cindy said coolly.

"We have to talk," he insisted urgently. "I mean all of us."

"We're on our way to lunch right now," Cindy pointed out. She started walking toward the door, with lanky Duffy right on her heels. "Let's talk there."

"No. We can't do that," Duffy argued, pushing the door open for her.

"Why not?" Cindy demanded, starting down the congested hall.

Duffy followed through the tangle of students, managing to hover over her continually. "Because Mollie will be there," he explained anxiously.

"You mean you don't want to talk in front of Mollie?" Cindy asked sweetly, her eyes hard with resentment. 'That's not a very good way to start a relationship, Duffy."

"I'm not sure what you mean, but I don't like the sounds of it at all."

"All right," Cindy conceded, running out of steam at the door to the cafeteria. "I agree that we do have to talk. But when?"

"After school, at my house," Duffy readily replied. "Grant and I have decided to hold our own little honesty hour. And I can tell you this. Cindy, we aren't going to be discussing the ups and downs of study hall."

Cindy stopped by the pool after school to tell Coach Lawford about her skin irritation. He excused her from practice for the required three days, but gruffly warned her against trying another facial. He needn't have bothered. Cindy had adamantly decided to leave all the primping to Mollie in the future.

"Well, hello, Cindy," Mrs. Duncan said fifteen minutes later, holding open the back screen door. "Duffy and the others are in the rumpus room waiting for you."

"Thanks, Mrs. Duncan," Cindy murmured, following Duffy's mother into her kitchen.

"I know I don't have to show you the way," Mrs. Duncan teased. "You've been down there almost as many times as I have."

Cindy was met with whoops and groans as she descended a short flight of stairs to the rumpus room on the lower level. Duffy and Grant were challenging Carey and Anna to a hot game of Ping-Pong.

"We won again!" Anna shouted, tossing her paddle into the air. She easily caught it again and danced gleefully around in a circle.

"Just don't jump over the net," Duffy snorted. "You might warp the table or something."

"Sore loser," Carey accused with a laugh.

"Cindy's here," Grant said, setting his paddle on the table.

"Great," Duffy said, rubbing his hands together. "Let's get started."

"Anna and Carey quickly sat down in the two wooden chairs against the wall, forcing Cindy to sit beside Grant on the plaid couch.

"Okay," Duffy said, pacing nervously around the room. "Who wants to begin?"

"I will," Grant said, running a hand through his curly black hair. "Cindy," he said in a no-nonsense tone, turning toward her. "I want to know why you're mad at me."

"Remember, Lewis, this is an honesty hour," Duffy put in.

"All right," Cindy retorted. "I'm mad, Grant, because you took off for the concert without me—"

"But Mollie said—"

"The concert that I gave you the ticket for!" Cindy continued, the anger simmering within her suddenly overflowing. "There I was, stuck at home wearing a sore rubber mask, and you didn't even have the courtesy to see how I was."

"But Mollie said you wouldn't want me to see you in that mask. She was sincerely trying to protect you, Cindy."

Cindy paused thoughtfully. "I guess that makes sense," she admitted. "In a Mollie sort of way."

"That should settle that," Grant said, kissing her lightly on the lips.

"I'll go next," Duffy said, his eyes nervously darting around the room.

"You should be on edge," Cindy scolded moving closer to Grant.

"What's the trouble between the two of you?" Carey asked, totally bewildered.

"I don't know what's on Cindy's mind," Duffy claimed, sitting down on the arm of the couch, his arms folded defensively across his chest.

"Hah!" Cindy cried. "Don't play innocent with me, Duncan. If this is really an honesty hour, I suggest you tell us where you stand with Mollie."

"Don't be mad before you know the facts," Duffy pleaded. "I need your help. Mollie's little crush on me has turned into a major mess." Duffy threw his hands up in a helpless gesture. "Don't get me wrong; I like the kid. But one minute I'm pulling her out of the ocean, the next minute she's permanently clamped on my arm like a watch!"

"Why are you complaining, buddy?" Grant wondered aloud. "You'll never be forced to wear another wrinkled shirt as long as you live!"

"As long as my mother's around anyway," Cindy added.

"I like being wrinkled," Duffy shot back. "I like being wrinkled and on the loose. One reason this group has stuck together so long is that none of you girls has pulled any lovey-dovey stuff on me."

"It's been tempting," Anna cooed playfully.

"It sure has," Carey agreed. "Wrinkled guys on the loose are hard to resist."

"I don't understand you, Duffy," Cindy said, growing serious. "You say you don't want to get involved with my sister, but you kissed her at the concert!"

"You did?" Carey squealed, clapping her hands together.

"Wow!" Anna said in burst of giggles.

"It's not like it seems," Duffy faltered.

"Mollie insists that you kissed her," Cindy maintained. "Don't you dare try to weasel out of it. We're all telling the truth."

Duffy reddened to the shade of an apple. "But you don't understand."

"A kiss is a kiss," Cindy said firmly.

"It wasn't a real kiss. Our lips ... just sort of collided."

"Oh?" Cindy raised a skeptical brow. "Mollie's over a foot shorter than you are. If you really had collided, she'd have planted one right on your rib cage."

"It all happened so fast. Everybody was standing up during one of Cyndi Lauper's rockin' songs, and I lifted Mollie into the air. Our faces were inches apart for a minute, and the rest is history."

Grant nodded in agreement. "That's exactly how it happened. As a matter of fact, it really took Duffy off guard. His lips were frozen in a pucker for the next half an hour."

Cindy sighed with relief. "I was hoping you'd come up with some crazy story to explain it."

"Gee, this honesty hour is going along great," Grant said, running his arm around Cindy's shoulders.

"It's not over yet," Carey said.

"No," Anna agreed, her tone now sober.

"What's the matter?" Cindy asked when she realized all of them were watching her.

"We wouldn't hurt Mollie for the world," Anna began.

"We think she's a sweet kid," Carey continued.

"But she doesn't belong in our group, Cindy," Grant told her gently.

Duffy flashed her an endearing smile. "Tell her, will ya, sport?"

"But how can I tell Mollie she's drummed out of the group?" Cindy wondered bleakly, glancing at her friends for an answer. "She'll be devastated."

"You do understand how we feel, don't you?" Grant asked.

"Of course I do," Cindy assured all of them. "I did some hard thinking yesterday and realized that Mollie and I were much better off when we each had our own friends."

"Having Mollie around seemed to work at first," Carey said. "But she has such a strong personality, and she does things so differently."

"We aren't holding the facial against her or anything," Anna said earnestly. "It was just a dumb accident, but why did she feel she had to impress us with that fancy gel in the first place?"

"She was just trying too hard and blew it," Cindy said, jumping to Mollie's defense. "But the bottom line is that she doesn't fit in as a permanent member of the gang. I let her tag along at first because we both sort of needed something to fill the empty space that Nicole left. But the whole thing snowballed when she totally dropped her friends. And then she fell for our redheaded wiseguy...."

"Maybe there is another way to give Mollie the message," Grant said thoughtfuly. "Mollie might turn against Cindy if she just blurts out the news."

"I think it would work out better if Mollie believes that leaving the group is her idea," Cindy proposed. "And believe me, she'll never give up Duffy just because I suggest it. She told me to mind my own business when I tried to discuss it with her the day of the rescue."

"Her interests are so different from ours," Duffy pointed out. "Maybe we should just start doing a lot of the things she hates to do. That should scare her off."

"Good idea," Cindy agreed, a mischievous grin sneaking across her face. "I think I know just the thing."

Chapter 11

While Cindy and her friends were discussing Mollie's fate, Mollie and Mrs. Lewis were at the Fabrics Plus store in the mall.

"I don't understand you, Mollie," Mrs. Lewis said, pausing near a display of colorful spools of thread. "You prepared for that Cyndi Lauper concert days in advance; then you turn around and put off an important homework assignment until the last minute."

"The concert was something to look forward to," Mollie explained defensively. "Making a dress for Sewing 201 is a total bummer."

"I would've thought you'd enjoy choosing the material for your dress. After all, you have such a flair for style."

"The whole assignment scares me to death!"

"Why can't you apply yourself at the sewing machine the way you do at the makeup table?"

"Sewing is so hard," Mollie groaned. "I only

took the class because I thought my good taste would make it a cinch."

"And you thought you could do anything that Heather can do," Mrs. Lewis added dryly.

Mollie nodded reluctantly. "That was part of it."

Mrs. Lewis held out her hand. "Give me the pattern so I know what we're dealing with."

Mollie dug into her purse and pulled out a square, dog-eared envelope smudged with lipstick and face powder.

"You have to be more careful with this envelope," Mrs. Lewis advised. "The pieces inside are only flimsy tissue paper."

"I know," Mollie said with exasperation. "I made that halter top, remember?"

"Ah, yes, I remember it well," Mrs. Lewis said as she examined the pattern. "No offense, dear, but I can't believe your teacher approved this complicated dress for a beginner like you. It has twenty-one pieces."

"It wasn't easy to convince her that I could handle it," Mollie confided in a huff.

"Why did you try?" Mrs. Lewis asked.

"I had to, Mom! We have to wear our work in a fashion show. Mrs. Young tried to unload dull stuff on all the beginners, but I had the sense to fight back! Can you imagine me parading around a stage in a smock?"

"I'm sure Mrs. Young measured your capabilities quite accurately," Mrs. Lewis argued.

"I'd rather die than appear in a fashion show wearing a hospital gown," Mollie vowed grimly.

Mrs. Lewis rolled her eyes. "I can't believe that Mrs. Young is letting you get away with this."

"I had to promise her that I had outside help on standby," Mollie confessed, toying with a spool of yellow thread.

Mrs. Lewis gasped in surprise and irritation. "Who's neck did you put on the line? Mine?"

"Not yours, Mom," Mollie said softly. "It's Heather's neck I used."

"You two aren't even on speaking terms!" Mrs. Lewis pointed out.

"Yeah." Mollie cast her a bleak look. "That's the worst part of it."

"A ticket to the Cyndi Lauper concert would have been a good start to mending the fence," Mrs. Lewis scolded.

"I know it," Mollie agreed. "But there weren't enough tickets to go around. If I gave a ticket to Heather, I would've had to give Sarah and Linda one, too. Then—then, Duffy wouldn't have been able to go. And then he wouldn't have ... It just wouldn't have worked out, that's all!"

"Maybe it isn't too late to get the smock pattern—"

"No! I wouldn't mind if we were just sewing it for a grade. I could have made the tacky smock and saved it for my next facial session with Cindy and the others."

Mrs. Lewis opened her mouth to protest, but clamped it shut again. There was no sense in telling Mollie in the middle of the fabric store that her facial business was out of business.

"But my reputation as a fashionable person is on the line here," Mollie continued frantically. "There's no time to fight about this, Mom. We're supposed to start sewing tomorrow. I have to cut out the pattern tonight!"

"All right," Mr. Lewis said wearily. "Let's look for some material."

Mother and daughter spent the next thirty minutes walking through the aisles examining the numerous bolts of fabric tightly lined up on the shelves like oversized books.

"I know a lot about clothing," Mollie said, slipping a bolt of bright-red-and-white polka-dot material back in place on a shelf. "After the pieces are sewn together, that is."

They finally settled for a lightweight blue poplin with narrow white stripes threaded through it.

Mollie took the bolt of poplin to the cutting table.

"What a lovely fabric!" the salesgirl exclaimed as she measured the required three and a half yards.

"We like it," Mrs. Lewis said. "The pattern is for a dress with a full skirt, so this poplin should look nice."

The girl nodded. "It seems like half the battle is over if you find the perfect material."

"It depends who has to fight the battle," Mollie replied. She glanced at her mother and they both began to laugh.

Grant showed up on the Lewises' doorstep at seven o'clock that evening.

"Why, Grant," Richard Lewis greeted him. "I had no idea you were coming by."

"I just thought I would surprise Cindy," he explained.

Mr. Lewis opened the door wider. "Come in, son!"

"Is Cindy busy?" he asked, looking beyond the foyer to the spacious living room.

"Yes, all my girls—except Nicole, of course—are working on a major project this evening."

"Oh." Grant looked crestfallen. "Maybe I should take off without bothering her."

"On the contrary, Grant," Mr. Lewis said over his shoulder as he headed for his easy chair in the living room, "I think Cindy would be very grateful for a diversion right about now. Go on back to the kitchen."

Grant entered the kitchen moments later to find Cindy, Mollie, and Mrs. Lewis hovering over the table.

"Don't cut anything yet!" Mrs. Lewis exclaimed.

"But we're ready," Mollie argued with scissors poised in the air.

"Looks like you're about to perform major surgery," Grant said, giving Cindy a quick hug.

"The patient's waiting on pins and needles," Cindy chirped, pointing to the large square of pale blue fabric with oddly shaped pieces of brown tissue paper pinned to it.

"Who's in charge?" he asked, his blue-green eyes sparkling with mischief.

"The girl with the scissors," Mollie promptly claimed.

"I am the one who bankrolled this venture," Mrs. Lewis objected. "And I say we hold off on the cutting for just a minute to double-check our pattern layout."

"I think I could use some fresh air," Cindy

announced. She took Grant's hand and led him toward the sliding glass door. "We'll be out back on the patio."

"Chicken," Mrs. Lewis called after her with a good-natured laugh.

Grant settled back on the wooden swing beside Cindy and slipped his arm around her shoulders.

"Your timing has never been better," Cindy said gratefully. "Except maybe when you're on your board doing a duck dive or a round house or something real showy."

"Hey, I aim to please," he chuckled. "Now, tell me how a surfer, a flirt, and a caterer ended up tackling a sewing project?"

Cindy went on to explain Mollie's predicament.

"Mollie *would* think making clothes is as simple as wearing them," Grant said, shaking his dark curly head in amusement.

The swing creaked as they leaned back.

"Just look at the stars up there," Grant said.

"Mmm, very romantic," Cindy murmured.

"It feels good to be alone for a change," Grant whispered huskily.

"Yeah." Cindy turned her head toward him, beaming affectionately.

Grant caught Cindy's chin in his free hand and pulled her face close to his. Her heart fluttered as he filled the small gap between them, brushing his lips against hers. He kissed her softly for a lingering moment, then continued with firm pressure. They finally broke apart with a sigh.

"I'm sorry, Cindy," he said softly, "about the concert mixup."

"It was disappointing for both of us," she replied, winding a short curl of his hair around her finger.

Grant grinned ruefully. "Going without you made for a pretty dull evening."

"So I heard," Cindy said, grinning back. "According to Mollie, you turned out to be quite the dud."

"That little shrimp!" he exploded.

"Don't take it too hard," Cindy advised. "It would've been impossible to compete with Mollie's one and only true love."

"I have to give her some credit," Grant said. "She is the only person we know who can unnerve the master of nerve."

"This whole romance thing is a new experience for Duffy," Cindy pointed out. "He's never been the object of a girl's affection before. I think he's flattered and confused at the same time. I'm just grateful that he hasn't come down hard on her."

"Yeah, he's been a real gentleman about it," Grant agreed with a mixture of disbelief and admiration.

They kissed again and then rocked back and forth for a while, enjoying the warm evening breeze.

"Do you think Mollie will take it very hard when she's dropped from the ranks?" Grant asked thoughtfully.

"She's going to dump us, remember?" Cindy shot him a crooked smile. "It's just a matter of time—with all of us working on her—until she realizes she's a square peg in our gang of beach bums."

"I suppose you're right," he conceded.

"I'd hate to see this go on much longer," Cindy said with a heavy sigh. "Mollie is so vulnerable when she has a crush on a guy. I just wouldn't want Duffy to lose his cool and tell her off."

"I know what you mean about crushes," Grant said, nodding his head. "I'm trying really hard to be patient and understanding with this girl I know who has a crush on me."

"Oh, yeah? Who's that?" Cindy asked seriously.

"Maybe you know her," Grant replied. "She's got short blond hair and a cute smile, and she's a mean surfer."

Cindy rewarded him with an elbow jab in the ribs.

"Yeow!" Grant yelled. He swiftly retailated by tickling her.

"What about trying to understand me?" Cindy asked between gulps of laughter. "What happened to all your patience?"

The sliding glass door opened suddenly, and Mrs. Lewis stepped outside. "Come inside, kids," she invited. "Were going to pop some corn in celebration. Mollie and I managed to cut out all the pattern pieces along the grain line!"

"I don't know what a grain line is, but I'm in favor of any celebration," Grant accepted eagerly. "And we know that Cindy's always in favor of eating...."

"You two can make the lemonade," Mrs. Lewis said before stepping back into the house.

"You're quite the joker tonight," Cindy said as Grant pulled her off the swing. "For a dud."

"Yeah, but my great kisses make up for all my faults," he said, lightly cuffing her under the chin as they headed for the house.

Chapter 12

"*R*ise and shine!" *Cindy said brightly, throw*ing back Mollie's bed covers.

"Huh?" Mollie blinked her eyes, scowled, and buried her face in her pillow.

"It's a beautiful Saturday morning," Cindy said in a singsong voice. "The sky is clear and the birds are singing."

"How do you know?" Mollie said, her voice muffled in the pillow.

"I just got back from a refreshing jog along the beach. Plenty of sunshine and water await us!"

"Await us when?"

"We're meeting the gang at the lifeguard station in an hour," Cindy replied. She pushed up the sleeves of her bright orange sweatshirt and gracefully bent over to touch her toes.

Mollie sat up in bed with effort. She rubbed her eyes and glanced at the clock to discover that it was barely eight-thirty. "Why do we have to go to the beach so early?"

"Because we want to get a good spot."

"Let the others save us a place," Mollie protested. "We only need a square foot or two."

"It's different this time. Duffy will need help setting up the volleyball net."

"Volleyball?" Mollie groaned in agony. "Oh, no."

"Oh, yes," Cindy said, touching her toes again to hide her amused expression. Today was the first step of their campaign to discourage Mollie with a physical workout, and already it seemed to be working. "We decided that it's about time we had another of our famous volleyball matches. You're still interested in coming along, aren't you?"

"I was planning to polish my nails out there," Mollie complained. "Fingers and toes."

"I wouldn't," Cindy advised. "Someone's liable to kick sand on your hands. Then you'd have a gritty mess."

"You're probably right," Mollie surrendered. "I'll do it when we get back."

"So you're going, then?"

"Sure, I wouldn't miss it for anything. Duffy would be so disappointed if I stayed away."

"Up, up, up," Cindy coaxed, clapping her hands together loudly. "Time to get the Lewis show on the road!"

Cindy was determined to keep Mollie on a hectic schedule and prodded her every step of the way. As a result of her persistence, they coasted up to the lifeguard station exactly an hour later.

Duffy and Grant were just crossing the sand with the volleyball equipment.

"Help has arrived!" Duffy greeted them happily.
The girls parked their bikes and joined them.

"Hi, Cin," Grant said with pleasure, kissing Cindy
lightly on the cheek.

"Hi, yourself," Cindy grinned and wrapped her
arms around his waist.

"You showed up just in time," Duffy said enthu-
siastically, flashing Mollie a huge smile.

"Really?" Mollie said, eyeing him flirtatiously.

"Come over here," Duffy invited daringly, wrig-
gling an eyebrow at Mollie.

Mollie sidled over to him, her fluffy blond ponytail swinging along with her hips. She stared
dreamily up into Duffy's eyes, her glossed lips on
the verge of a large pucker. Suddenly she felt cold
metal in her hands.

"Carry this pole, will ya, kid?" he asked innocently.

"But—but," she sputtered. Why couldn't he fol-
low Grant's lead and give her a kiss, she wondered with disgust.

"I'll get my board and the beach bags," Cindy
volunteered hastily to cut off any protests from
Mollie.

"To the shore, troops!" Duffy hollered, swinging a muscular arm in the direction of the sea.

The foursome found a nice open spot near the
shore. While the guys worked on the volleyball
net, Cindy and Mollie spread Duffy's beach blanket out on the sand.

"Come help us out, girls," Grant called, driving
one of the poles into the sand.

Cindy quickly stripped off her clothes down to
her green tank suit and scampered through the
hot sand to pull the net up into the air.

Mollie slowly slipped off her lacy coverup, revealing the yellow bikini that had given her so much grief during her surfing lesson. Without a glance at the workers, she sat daintily down on the blanket and dug into her beach bag.

"Mollie, a little help over here," Cindy called out.

"Not until I'm covered with sunscreen," she declared, waving a white plastic bottle in the air.

Cindy and the guys groaned as they pretended to struggle with the equipment.

"Just because you don't take care of your skin, doesn't mean I have to make the same mistake." Mollie busily rubbed the lotion on her sleek limbs.

"We use suntan lotion and zinc oxide," Cindy shot back.

"It's sort of important that we get this net set up while there's still room for it," Duffy added impatiently.

"I have to do what I have to do," Mollie insisted, squeezing more lotion into the palm of her hand.

"Here come Carey and Anna," Grant observed, gesturing toward the lifeguard station.

Cindy followed his gaze and spotted the girls, carrying a cooler between them.

"They got the chow?" Duffy asked, concentrating on the net.

"They got the chow," Cindy said, imitating his voice.

Carey and Anna assisted with the net, and within minutes the five of them were volleying the ball back and forth under the brilliant blue sky.

"C'mon, Mollie!" Duffy urged with a wave. "Grant and I can't take these girls on alone."

Mollie reluctantly stood up and joined them in the sand.

"Here," Duffy said, shooting the ball into Mollie's stomach. "You serve."

Mollie grunted as the ball made impact with her gut, but her face held determination. She could do anything they could do. But Mollie soon found that desire wasn't always enough. She tossed the ball in the air and punched it awkwardly with her fist. It popped forward, struck the net, and bounced back at her team, landing at Grant's feet.

Cindy, Carey, and Anna snickered as the boys growled in frustration.

"Maybe you should hold your miniature player up a foot or two when she serves," Anna suggested.

"Give the kid a chance," Grant said. "She's still young and inexperienced."

Their remarks took immediate effect on Mollie. She stuck her lip out poutingly and narrowed her eyes to slits. "Give me the ball again," she demanded.

"I'll serve this time," Duffy said in a fatherly tone. Grant tossed him the ball and he twirled it on the tip of his finger. Mollie said nothing but stubbornly stayed in the game.

They volleyed the ball back and forth once again, purposely keeping it out of petite Mollie's reach.

"Hit it to me," Mollie commanded, finally running out of patience.

Anna slapped the ball in her direction. Mollie lost her nerve as the ball shot over the net, and she instinctively raised her hands in front of her face. The ball landed with the accuracy of a missile, hitting the tips of her fingers.

"Ouch!" she screamed, gently examining her sore hands finger by finger.

"Sorry, Mollie," Anna called out with real concern. "You should've jumped out of the way if it was too much."

"You okay, Mollie?" Cindy asked, ducking under the net to check her sister's hands.

"Two of my nicest fingernails broke!" Mollie snapped. "I hate this game," she muttered, stomping off in a huff.

"Let's all take a breather," Grant suggested.

Everyone sat on the blanket together, and Carey passed out cans of pop and sandwiches. They relaxed together in the hot sun, exchanging good-natured banter while watching the surfers test their skill on the rough waves.

"Let's show 'em how it's done," Duffy said suddenly to Cindy, setting his half-eaten sandwich back in the cooler for safekeeping.

Cindy swallowed a mouthful of food and looked at him blankly. "Now?"

"Now," he insisted, pulling her to her feet.

"Are you trying to get me alone?" Cindy teased, as she and Duffy paddled out beyond the breaking waves.

"Yeah," Duffy admitted in a nervous voice.

They didn't speak again until they'd reached the surf line. They turned their boards around so that they were in position to catch one of the powerful swells that had been rolling in from the distance quite routinely that day.

"Cindy, do you think Mollie's over me yet?" Duffy asked, his face full of hope.

"Well, I don't know for sure...." Cindy teased

thoughtfully as small waves gently rocked their boards like a couple of cradles. "You're pretty irresistible. It might take all afternoon to scare her off."

"Nuts," Duffy griped, knocking his knuckles on his fiberglass board in frustration.

"Here comes the big one," Cindy announced excitedly, watching it approach over her shoulder.

With expert timing, Cindy and Duffy began to paddle until their speed matched that of the breaking water. In unison, they rose to full height, extending their arms like graceful wings. Accustomed to each other's methods of operation, they managed to ride the wave together and glide in for a smooth landing.

"Great job," Grant said, meeting Cindy on the shore with his surfboard in hand.

"You should've come along," Cindy said, pulling her board out of the foamy water.

"I knew Duffy wanted to talk to you, so I sat this one out. Is he on edge because of Mollie?"

"Yeah, what else," Cindy said, glancing at Duffy a few feet away talking to a boy from school.

"Ready for another shot at it?" Grant asked, stepping into the water.

"No," Cindy said, eyeing Mollie seated on the blanket filing her nails and wearing a grumpy expression. "I think I'll sit with the girls for a while."

"Are you hogging my boyfriend?" Mollie whispered in her sister's ear the moment Cindy sat down on the blanket.

"No!" Cindy denied, taken aback by Mollie's accusation. She pointed to Duffy, paddling his way back out to sea with Grant. "He's nowhere near me."

"He's going out again?" Mollie said indignantly, filing her index finger with a vengeance.

"Duffy isn't the type to lounge around on the sand," Cindy said, dabbing her face with a towel.

"Both sides are supposed to give in a relationship," Mollie argued.

"Duffy's pretty set in his ways," Anna put in.

"Yeah, he's about as flexible as a two-by-four," Carey chimed in.

"But I'm his girlfriend. . . ." Mollie protested, her round blue eyes full of faith.

Cindy and her friends exchanged significant glances.

"Has he ever said that you're his girlfriend?" Cindy asked bluntly.

"No, not yet," Mollie admitted with a disappointed sigh.

"How long are you willing to wait?" Carey wondered.

Cindy nodded. "Are you willing to sit out here in the hot sun week after week watching him play volleyball and surf?"

"Nothing is like I thought it would be," Mollie grumbled, rising to her feet. "I'm going wading to cool off."

"Is she ever headstrong," Anna said, shaking her head.

"She just has to learn to save her spunk for the right causes," Cindy said with a worried frown.

Chapter 13

"*Who* is on the phone, Cindy?" Mollie scooted out of her bedroom on Sunday morning in a royal blue swimsuit, brushing her hair as she moved.

Cindy, standing in the hall in her red-and-white T-shirt and faded cutoffs, raised a finger to her lips and continued listening intently into the receiver. "Okay, see you then." She hung up and grinned at her sister. "That was Duffy."

"Did he ask for me?" she asked anxiously. "You could've hollered. I was awake."

"We were making plans for this afternoon," Cindy explained. "The guys are coming over here."

"You mean it'll be just the four of us?" Mollie squealed.

"Yes, but take it easy," Cindy said. "You might not—"

"Super!" Mollie jumped up and down waving the brush like a banner.

"We're going to—" Cindy began, only to be cut short again.

"Play records? Dance? Get a couple of movies for the VCR?"

"Mollie—"

"We could have a Tom Cruise marathon. *Top Gun. The Color of Money.*" Mollie began to pace up and and down the hallway, her brain ticking away like mad. "I could forget about my diet just for today, I suppose. We could make some tacos. Maybe onion rings, too. We really should clean up the family room a little bit, too," she added.

"If you really want to help, you could sweep the garage," Cindy said, jumping into the one-sided conversation the second that Mollie took a breath.

"What?" Mollie stopped in her tracks, wearing a bewildered frown. "I don't get it."

"We're going to wax our surfboards out in the garage," Cindy answered patiently.

"You can't mean it! That won't be any fun!"

"It'll be fun for us," Cindy assured her.

"It'll be just as dull as the beach was yesterday." Mollie moped. "You'll all be busy, and I'll have to sit around and watch."

"We're just being ourselves," Cindy shot back. "You're just used to doing different things with your own friends."

"At least they knew how to have a good time." Mollie hung her head in disappointment.

Cindy watched her anxiously, hoping Mollie would give in and call Heather or one of her other old friends. She was tempted to suggest it, but knew it would work out much better if Mollie made the decision on her own.

Mollie raised her head with extreme effort, forcing a brave smile. "If the gang's going to be in the garage, I'll be there, too."

The Lewises' garage was a hub of activity two hours later. The air was filled with music, laughter, and the smell of wax. Cindy and the guys had positioned their boards on sawhorses covered with old blankets for padding. Then they'd begun the first step of roughing up the old coat of wax on their boards with wax combs and dusting the flakes away. The final step of the process was to rub a mixture of paraffin and beeswax on the fiberglass surface.

Mollie stubbornly sat on a step stool a couple of feet away from Duffy, her chin resting in her hand, her small foot tapping to the beat of the music on the radio.

"Is it really so important to doll up those boards that way?" she asked skeptically, thinking of the fun they could have had in the Lewis family room.

"This isn't a beauty treatment, Mollie," Duffy answered in a preoccupied tone as he rubbed wax on the board in a circular motion with a rag. "It gives a surfer the traction he needs."

"Or the traction *she* needs," Cindy put in, glancing up from her work to grin at him.

"Hey, Duffy," Grant said, grabbing a new rag from a pile on the workbench. "Whatever happened to your creative communication extra-credit assignment?"

Duffy laughed with satisfaction. "I wrapped it up just like that!" he claimed, snapping his fingers.

"I don't believe it!" Cindy gasped in amazement. "I walked over hot coals to come up with my honesty hour."

Grant nodded in agreement. "How could you dream up something so easily? You aren't exactly the scholarly type."

"My idea came naturally." He pointed to Cindy's boom box on the workbench. "I asked myself, 'Duncan my man, what does communication mean to you?' The first thing that popped into my head was my favorite rockin' radio station, WOWE."

"What are you going to do?" Grant taunted. "Turn on Wowie for an hour? Mr. Thomas will blow a circuit."

Duffy shook his bright red head, smiling broadly. "My plan is nothing as simpleminded as that. I've summoned the king of WOWE himself, Stan Sting. He's agreed to speak to our class tomorrow about his life as a disk jockey."

"You actually talked to the Stinger?" Mollie gushed, nearly swooning off her chair.

"Yep. I went down to Wowie in person and set up the deal. Mr. Thomas almost swallowed his chalk when I told him about it on Friday. You know, I don't think he thought I could pull it off."

"How could you keep this news to yourself?" Cindy demanded.

"I wanted to watch your faces when he strutted into the class tomorrow. But I just couldn't keep it a secret anymore."

"Is his hair really green?" Mollie asked breathlessly.

Duffy shrugged. "It was hard to tell for sure if it was green or blue, but I think it did look more green."

"Knock heads with him, Duffy, and the two of you will look like a traffic light," Cindy teased, her green eyes dancing with merriment.

"Very funny," Duffy muttered. "You guys should be calling me a genius or something."

"Okay," Grant relented. "Hey, genius, let's go try out our new wax jobs on some tubes."

"Now you're talkin'," Duffy agreed, tossing aside his rag.

"Let's stay here instead," Mollie pleaded, batting her heavily shadowed eyes at Duffy in an effort to sway him.

"Don't you want to take another shot at a curl?" Duffy challenged.

"No, I don't, Duffy Duncan!" Mollie lashed back angrily. "You never compromise and do the things I want to do. All you care about is the beach." Mollie hopped off the step stool and stood facing him defiantly, her arms folded across her chest.

Cindy flashed Grant a significant look and tossed her head in the direction of the open garage door. He raised a brow in question, but followed her out to the driveway.

"What gives?" he asked, shoving his hands into the pockets of his worn cutoffs.

"I think Mollie's about to break off with Duffy."

"Oh." Grant grinned with new understanding. "How about a snack while we wait?"

"Good idea. Mom brought home some cream puffs yesterday from Moveable Feasts. Let's go grab a few from the fridge and eat them out here so we can listen in."

"Good idea. Race ya," Grant challenged, darting off as he spoke.

"All you care about is the beach," Mollie repeated, now looking more crestfallen than indignant.

"You're right, Mollie. I care a lot about the beach. But you've known that all along. I've been hanging around your house for years."

"But, I thought ... that maybe you'd change, try some of the things I like to do."

"I am happy with the way my life is now, Mol," Duffy explained, studying the toe of his worn running shoe with intense interest. "I guess I don't want to change the way I do things."

Mollie took a fortifying breath. "I hope you're going to understand what I have to say, Duffy. What I'd like to say ..."

"You can tell me anything, Mollie," Duffy urged.

There was an uncomfortable silence as Mollie struggled to find the right words. "I really appreciate the way you came to my rescue in the ocean," she began. "And I had a wonderful time at the Cyndi Lauper concert." Mollie reddened as she relived the wonderful kiss between them. Duffy reddened a little, too, and busily screwed the cover back on the jar of wax. "It was one of the best dates I ever had."

Duffy opened his mouth to object to the word date, but clamped it shut again.

Mollie threw her arms up in frustration. "Oh, Duffy, no matter how much we want to be a couple, it just wouldn't work out between us. We have to face it. We have absolutely nothing in common. We don't belong together!"

"I'll say we don't," Duffy agreed fervently.

"You didn't have to agree so fast," Mollie objected in a hurt tone.

"What I mean is, we tried it and it didn't work out," Duffy amended. "It's too bad, Mollie. You're nice. And pretty, too."

Cindy raced back to the driveway with Grant just in time to hear Duffy's last remarks. "Why doesn't he just shut up and let Mollie dump him?" she whispered, sinking her teeth into a second cream puff.

Grant wiped away a dot of cream on her nose and grinned. "Duffy can't resist putting on a show. Ever."

"He may just end up with a steady girlfriend if he spreads it on too thick."

Mollie was aglow under Duffy's complimentary gaze. "Maybe we should try a little harder to make our love work."

Duffy gulped. "No, I think you were right to cut things off now. You don't like to hang around the beach, and I can't get into the mall scene. That really leaves us at a dead end."

"It was fun while it lasted," Mollie murmured.

"Friends?" Duffy extended his hand.

"The best of friends," Mollie agreed. slipping her hand in his.

Cindy gave Grant a nod, and together they walked into the garage, just as if they'd been gone all along.

"Let's load my car, Grant, and head for the beach," Duffy said, examining his wax job with pride.

Grant turned to Cindy. "You coming along?"

"Yeah, in a minute."

The boys hoisted their boards over their heads and walked out of the garage.

"Are you okay, Mollie?" Cindy hovered over her with a concerned expression.

"Yeah. It's all over between Duffy and me."

"I'm sure it's for the best," Cindy said encouragingly.

"Yeah. I realize now that I don't belong with Duffy, or any of your crowd." Mollie smiled sadly. "Losing Nicole to Boston was so hard. I thought if we stuck together, we'd miss her less."

"I did, too," Cindy admitted. "But I think we can still be close, even if we go our separate ways sometimes."

"Guess I'm sort of left with no one."

"You could get your old friends back," Cindy suggested.

"They've probably forgotten all about me by now," Mollie lamented.

Cindy felt a wave of compassion for her sister. "Tell you what, I'll forget about the beach for today. We still have time to rent a video."

"No, go ahead," Mollie said with a sniff. "I want to be alone." With that she brushed past Cindy and darted through the door into the house.

Duffy's guest speaker, Stan Sting from the radio station WOWE, gave an interesting lecture on radio broadcasting to the creative communication class on Monday morning. Near the end of the hour, the Stinger, as he was known to all his fans, set aside time to autograph his promotional photos for all the students.

Cindy sat at her desk until the line thinned out.

When she did finally get near Mr. Thomas's desk, where the Stinger was perched, Duffy was in the process of handing him a third picture.

"Dedicate this one to Mollie," he requested. "She spells it with *ie* instead of a *y*. Oh, yeah, you better put 'love' on there someplace. She's really hung up on the stuff."

The skinny man with the spiked green hair smiled understandingly at Duffy. "I always wish the girls lots of love, Duffy." He began to scrawl a message to Mollie in large, sweeping strokes.

"Hi, there," Cindy said, tapping her pal on the shoulder.

Duffy jumped at her touch. "Hey, it's not fair to sneak up on a guy," he scolded, looking uncomfortable.

"I heard you just now," she told him.

"I figured you did," Duffy retorted, shifting uncomfortably from one foot to another.

"I just want you to know how nice I think it is for you to remember Mollie."

"Who could forget her?" Duffy rolled his eyes, accepting the picture from the Stinger. "Thanks, man—I mean for coming, and everything."

"Thanks for asking me. Gives me an air of respectability." Stan Sting grinned and took Cindy's picture.

"Make this out to Cindy," she requested. "With a *y*."

"Is this your girlfriend, Duffy?" the disk jockey asked with a crooked grin.

"No way!" Duffy's denial was quick. "I'm a free spirit, a hunk on the loose, just like you."

The Stinger leaned forward slightly. "Don't let

it get around," he confided, "but I'm married and have a kid in the eighth grade."

"You look so young!" Duffy's disappointment was obvious.

The Stinger shrugged. "Dying your hair green really throws people off the track."

Mr. Thomas joined them a moment later. "Uh, Mr. Stinger," he ventured, looking ill at ease with the free spirit. "I would like to thank you for coming...." Cindy and Duffy exchanged a silent look and moved over to the windows near Grant.

"I'll give Mollie her picture at lunch," Duffy said, slipping it into his folder.

"I got her a picture, too," Grant informed him with irritation.

"I'm sure she'll appreciate both of them," Cindy consoled, patting each boy on the back.

"Mine has 'love' on it," Duffy favored Grant with a superior look.

"So does mine," Grant shot back.

"It'll take more than a couple of pictures to cheer Mollie up, I'm afraid." Cindy gazed out of the window with a worried expression. "She feels so alone. She's let us go, and her friends aren't speaking to her."

"That's rough," Duffy agreed. "I feel so responsible. After all, it was my good looks and personality that caused all the trouble."

"I think the trouble is sister trouble," Cindy corrected. "If only we could somehow reunite Mollie with Heather and Linda and Sarah," Cindy continued thoughtfully. "I know if they were forced to face each other, the deep freeze would thaw in no time."

"Wouldn't it be nice if everyone showed up at your swim meet after school today?" Duffy grinned mischievously.

"How could you possibly arrange that?" Cindy's green eyes were wide with disbelief.

Duffy ignored her question and turned to Grant. "Grant, you're going to be covering the meet for the yearbook, right?"

Grant eyed him suspiciously. "Yeah, Jim Spear and I are coming to take some pictures and talk to the swimmers. So?"

Duffy shrugged evasively. "A little white lie here and a trick or two there should take care of it."

Chapter 14

*C*indy always felt a little nervous and excited just before a swim meet. But as she stepped out into the pool area that afternoon after school, she felt something more: anxiety. Mollie hadn't shown up in the cafeteria for lunch, and considering how sad she was about being lost between her sophomore friends and junior ones, Cindy couldn't help worrying.

What if Mollie had skipped her classes and fled to the mall, her home away from home? Wherever she was, Cindy was sure the news was bad.

With one last shred of hope, Cindy scanned the rapidly filling bleachers for a glimpse of Mollie's bright yellow knit dress. After all, Mollie had promised to attend this first meet of the year to cheer her on. But, Cindy reminded herself, that promise was made before Mollie's talk with Duffy in the garage yesterday. Cindy's heart sank when there was no sign of her among the spectators.

"Lewis!" Coach Lawford bellowed between cupped hands.

"I'm going in now," Cindy called back above the drone of the crowd and the sound of churning water.

"Don't get wet!"

"Huh?" Cindy stared back at the coach with surprise, noticing suddenly that only members of the opposing team from Newport Beach were warming up in the pool. Her Vista teammates were clustered together near the wall under the large clock.

"Get over here on the double!"

Cindy scurried across the slippery wet tiles and joined her friends.

The coach blew his whistle to get their attention. "A couple of people from the yearbook staff are coming any minute to cover this meet. Darn nuisance, if you ask me," he muttered half under his breath. "Anyway, the photographer wants to take a group picture now and some candid shots during competition."

"Here they come, Coach," Jane Leonard said as the boys' locker room door swung open.

When Cindy saw Grant armed with a notebook, and Jim Spear right on his heels carrying a camera, she suddenly remembered that Grant had mentioned that he was covering the meet for the yearbook.

Since Coach Lawford was glowering at the two boys, ordering them to hurry, Grant only paused to favor Cindy with a quick wink before proceeding to ask the burly man some questions. Jim Spear, visibly nervous under the stress, aimed his camera at the group with a shaky hand.

Spear doesn't know what real trouble is, Cindy thought ruefully. He should be faced with the case of a missing sister. This is real stress!

"Enough shutterbugging and interviewing for now! Hit the water for warm-ups!" Coach Lawford turned his back on the girls as the Newport coach approached him.

Grant sidled over to Cindy.

"What are you so uptight about?" Grant asked, pretending to jot down notes in his book in case the coach was watching.

"Mollie is still missing," Cindy explained in a nervous rush.

"She isn't really missing," Grant disagreed. "You just haven't seen her."

"Have you seen her? Has anyone?"

"Come to think of it," Grant said thoughtfuly, "I did see her this afternoon between fifth and sixth period."

"Did you talk to her?" Cindy asked anxiously.

"No. I wasn't close enough. But I know it was Mollie," Grant hastened to assure her. "She had on that yellow dress that makes her look like a canary."

Cindy sighed with relief. "At least she was here at Vista where she belonged."

"Of course she was here," Grant said in a reassuring tone.

"But where was she at lunchtime?" Cindy wondered. "And where is she now?"

"I don't know about Mollie, but it looks like

Duffy managed to round up everyone else," Grant said, pointing to the top row of the bleachers.

Cindy followed Grant's gaze, to find Duffy climbing up the bleachers, followed by Mollie's old gang, like a mother duck leading her chicks. She could see the girls chattering away with Duffy and pointing to her and Grant as they took their seats.

"I wonder what Duffy told the girls to lure them to this meet," Grant said with a chuckle. "He looks pretty uncomfortable sitting with three giggly girls."

Cindy sighed and pulled her goggles over her eyes. "We'll find out soon enough."

"Forget about your troubles and get out there and do your stuff, champ."

"Thanks."

"I'd kiss you for luck, but then I'd have to kiss all the girls I interview for the yearbook." Grant's blue-green eyes danced with merriment.

Cindy turned and dove into the water, making certain to splash Grant and his notepad.

An hour and a half later the Vista High swimmers had proven once again that they were the champs. Cindy had placed first in the breaststroke, first in the freestyle, and second in the hundred-meter backstroke.

Grant and Jim had been seated on a bench at poolside during the entire meet, jotting down highlights and taking candid shots. Now that the meet was over, Grant began to circulate among the Vista girls for brief interviews.

As the spectators streamed out of the exits, Duffy and the sophomore girls inched their way down to the pool area as well. Before Cindy knew what was happening, the four of them had boxed her in a tight square.

"Hi, Cindy," Heather said excitedly.

"We're ready," Linda said eagerly.

"Thanks a lot," Sarah chimed in. "Duffy says you set it up."

"Duffy said that?" Cindy asked sharply, turning to Duffy with a curious glare.

"You know, Cin," Duffy said with a quick wink. "The girls have agreed to pose as fans of the swim team for the yearbook pictures."

"Yeah, we sat through the entire meet so we'd have the chance," Heather informed her, glowing with anticipation.

"Let me talk to Duffy alone for a second," Cindy requested, clamping a firm hand on his arm.

The girls exchanged doubtful glances.

"Everything is okay, isn't it?" Linda asked. "We can look excited about swimming, honest. Just stick us in the crowd and we'll say cheese." Linda demonstrated with a huge toothy smile.

"I'm sure you could do it," Cindy said, pulling Duffy several feet away.

To Cindy's surprise, Duffy had the nerve to act annoyed. "Okay, Cindy, so where is Mollie? I go to all the trouble of rounding up her goofy little friends and she doesn't even show up. I clearly remember your telling me she planned to be here this afternoon."

"I don't know where Mollie is," Cindy said, now more worried than ever. "But, Duffy, how could you lie to those girls—in my name yet! I can't get them into yearbook pictures."

"I didn't think that far ahead," Duffy explained in exasperation. "I expected Mollie to be here. I expected the girls to hug and squeal and ask me to drive them over to the mall."

Cindy glanced over at the threesome waiting for them impatiently. "Oh, no, here come Grant and Jim. And look, Duffy, Heather and the others are going toward them!"

Cindy rushed over to try to referee, dragging the reluctant Duffy along.

"Here we are!" Heather, Linda, and Sarah chorused, nearly tackling the yearbook representatives.

Grant and Jim exchanged puzzled looks.

"Let me explain," Cindy said without much enthusiasm.

"Something's fishy here," Heather muttered.

"You are going to take our picture, aren't you?" Linda asked Jim.

"We're here covering the meet," Jim said.

"But we wanted to be in the pictures," Sarah objected.

"If you want to be in the yearbook, go join a club, like stagehands or chess. I haven't taken their pictures yet."

"Why, you crummy shutterbug!" Linda flared.

They all began to chatter at once. Cindy finally whistled sharply to get their attention. "Duffy—all of us, really, were hoping to get you together with Mollie this afternoon," she explained.

"You mean Duffy made up the picture deal?" Heather demanded angrily.

"What a jerk!" Linda snapped.

"Mollie was supposed to be at the meet," Cindy

continued, "and Duffy thought if he could gather you together, you could work out your differences."

"Hang 'em high!" Sarah shouted, glaring at Duffy.

Duffy gulped, wondering how he had ever got involved with the crazy mob of girls in the first place.

"I admit Duffy went overboard," Cindy said apologetically. "But we were desperate to help Mollie out. She's finally realized she doesn't belong with our crowd, but doesn't know how to tell you she's sorry for the way she treated you."

"Where is Mollie?" Heather asked, looking around.

"I don't know for sure," Cindy replied. "She never showed up. I'm really worried about her."

"Maybe we should spread out and look for her," Heather suggested, to Cindy's delight.

"This isn't another trick, is it?" Linda asked Duffy.

Duffy instinctively jumped back a step. "My bag of tricks is empty, honest."

"I'll go to the locker room and change my clothes," Cindy proposed. "Let's meet out in the hall in ten minutes."

"In the meantime I'll call your house to see if she headed for home," Grant offered.

"Thanks." Cindy kissed Grant quickly on the lips and headed for the locker room.

"No answer at your house," Grant told Cindy a short time later, when she joined the group in the hall.

"I knew that would be too easy an answer," Cindy groaned.

After a brief discussion the group decided to

AND THEN THERE WERE TWO   125

comb the school before branching out to the mall and Pete's Pizzeria. They broke up into pairs and took off in different directions. Heather offered to join Cindy.

"We've really missed Mollie," Heather told her as the two of them checked classrooms one by one.

"I know she misses you, too," Cindy replied. "But her pride sometime gets in her way."

Cindy and Heather finally ended up in the wing of the school that housed the vocational classrooms.

"What's that hum?" Heather asked, pausing to listen.

"Maybe somebody's tinkering around with a small engine," Cindy suggested.

"Maybe," Heather agreed, walking ahead to the last room in the wing. She peered around the doorway. "Here she is!"

Of course, Cindy thought as she jogged down the hall. The home economics room! I forget about Mollie's sewing project!

Mollie, seated at the sewing machine, heard voices and took her foot off the floor pedal. "What's going on?" she asked as Heather, then Cindy, rushed into the classroom.

"We've been looking all over for you!" Cindy scolded with a mixture of relief and irritation.

"What did you think?" Mollie asked, "that I skipped school or something?"

"No, of course not," Cindy lied. "But you skipped lunch, and you skipped my meet!"

"Sorry," Mollie said, not sounding too sincere. "But I'm in a real jam with this crazy dress! I've been at this machine every free minute today! Mrs. Young announced this morning that she's scheduled the fashion show for next Saturday afternoon."

"Hello, girls." Mrs. Young breezed into the room with an armload of papers. She set the papers on her desk and approached Mollie's machine. "Oh, it's you, Heather," she said, adjusting the glasses on her nose. "To tell you the truth, dear," she clucked, shaking her gray head, "I was beginning to doubt Mollie's word."

"What?" Heather stared at her in confusion.

"I allowed Mollie to take on this complicated pattern only because she said you, one of my best ex-pupils, were willing to offer her guidance. But quite frankly, Heather, I've yet to see any of your seamstress skills on this dress."

Mollie's throat tightened until she could barely swallow as Heather stared at her in amazement.

"Heather?" Mrs. Young prodded. "What do you have to say?"

Heather cleared her throat, prolonging Mollie's agony. Why doesn't she just blurt out the truth? Mollie wondered. It didn't matter anymore. She knew she'd never be able to complete the assignment on her own.

"I've been pretty busy, Mrs. Young," Heather finally replied. "But if Mollie wants to bring the dress over to my house a few nights this week, I'm sure we can get the job done."

"I'd love to!" Mollie cried, jumping up to hug Heather over the machine.

"My, what an outpouring of affection," Mrs.

Young declared, staring at the two misty-eyed girls. "You'd think this was a reunion!"

Cindy sighed happily. "You know how kids are, Mrs. Young. Always worked up over something."

Mrs. Young patted Cindy on the back. "I don't recall ever seeing you in one of my sewing classes."

Cindy reddened. "No. I'm not the type."

"Well, you think about it for next semester," she suggested. "I have to run to the office for a moment. Mollie, feel free to work here another half an hour."

"How generous," Mollie grumbled, after the teacher left. She reluctantly sat down at the machine again.

"I'm going to tell everybody that we found you," Cindy said. "I advise the two of you to talk things over."

"I really think you should let us work this out," Mollie told her sister in a patient tone. "We decided to be more independent of each other, remember? The way we were before Nicole left."

Independent? Cindy was tempted to point out that she'd just delivered Heather, a good friend and expert seamstress, to self-sufficient Mollie's side! But on second thought, Cindy decided to let it go. Heather was already standing behind Mollie's sewing chair, trying to make sense of the ball of fabric bunched up on the machine. There was nothing like a crisis to bring friends together.

Cindy found everyone milling around outside near the steps of the school. "Mollie was here all along," she announced. "She's been holed up in the home economics room working on her dress."

"Figures," Duffy said.

"Let's go check it out, Sarah," Linda said. They dashed up the steps giggling and disappeared through the school entrance.

"They giggle about everything," Duffy said, shaking his head in awe.

"Let's go get a breath of salt air," Grant suggested, slipping his arm around Cindy's shoulders.

"A walk along the beach would be nice," Cindy agreed.

"Is this a romantic thing, or can I come along?" Duffy asked dryly.

"Come on, Duncan," Grant invited. "My conscience wouldn't allow me to leave you behind with those girls. That rowdy bunch would chew you up and spit you out in a matter of minutes."

Chapter 15

"*I'm hemming as fast as I can, Mollie!*"

Mollie was standing on a wooden stool in her bedroom while Heather, seated at her feet with needle and thread, tried hastily to shorten Mollie's blue dress for the school fashion show.

"Mrs. Young will kill me if I'm late," Mollie said mournfully, glancing at her watch. "She's been on my case ever since the first day of class."

"I don't understand why you had to have the dress an inch shorter," Heather complained. "It looked fine to me."

"My knees weren't showing," Mollie reminded her for what seemed like the tenth time. "The school auditorium is going to be jammed with people. I want to look just right."

"I could've hemmed a lot faster if you'd taken the dress off," Heather griped.

"I thought we'd save time this way," Mollie shot back. "Some sewing tutor you've turned out to be!"

"Ingrate!"

"Ouch! You poked me in the leg on purpose."

"Prove it."

Cindy and Mrs. Lewis, who were standing together in the hallway eavesdropping, exchanged satisfied smiles.

"Sounds like things are back to normal," Cindy observed in a whisper.

"Music to my ears," Mrs. Lewis happily agreed.

Thirty minutes later Mollie, Cindy, and Heather breezed through the backstage door of the Vista High auditorium. The dressing rooms were a hubbub of activity, and the air was filled with female chatter. Mothers scurried around with makeup kits and outfits on hangers. Girls flew around in slips and fancy shoes. Mrs. Young walked the floors with a clipboard and a mug of coffee, firing off directions.

"You better go get a seat in the auditorium while you still have the chance, Cindy," Mollie instructed, dumping her cosmetic bag out on a table already littered with makeup. "Heather is going to stay back here and assist Mrs. Young."

"Okay," Cindy agreed. "Mom and Dad are waiting for me out there someplace."

Mr. Lewis's face looked forlorn as Cindy slipped into the empty seat between her parents. "Another model in the family," he was saying to his wife.

"But you're proud of Nicole's modeling," Mrs. Lewis pointed out with a grin.

"Of course! I'm proud of all my girls," he said, winking at Cindy. "But the three of them always seem to be in the limelight."

"So?" Laura Lewis inquired. "It shows they have initiative."

"Yes, but one of these days three guys are going to come along and notice them. Then they'll run off and get married and leave me all alone."

"Not before you pay for huge, elaborate weddings," Mrs. Lewis teased.

Mr. Lewis cast a sly look at his wife. "I'll get by cheap. I know a wonderful caterer who will work for nothing!"

Mrs. Lewis leaned over Cindy to rap her husband on the arm with her rolled up program, just as the curtains were opening on stage.

"Welcome to our fashion show," Mrs. Young said from a podium at the side of the stage.

A round of applause swept through the auditorium. Cindy heard a familiar whistle in the crowd and turned around, to find Duffy, Grant, Carey, and Anna standing against the back wall. They really do care about Mollie, she thought with satisfaction. Even if she is a pain in the neck sometimes.

Upbeat music came over the PA system, and Mrs. Young announced the name of the first model. As each model took her turn on stage, Mrs. Young described the outfit and the seamstress.

"When is Mollie coming on?" Mr. Lewis asked impatiently forty-five minutes later.

"Next," Cindy whispered. She was also getting anxious. She knew how much this fashion show meant to her sister.

A moment later Cindy and her parents riveted their attention to the stage as Mollie moved gracefully across in her full-skirted blue-and-white dress.

Her long blond hair was curled in ringlets and captured in a white satin ribbon, and she wore a new pair of sophisticated white pumps.

"It's hard to believe that this is the same piece of fabric that Mollie and I bought at the mall," Mrs. Lewis exclaimed with pride.

"I understand now why Mollie didn't want to wear one of those smocks on stage," Cindy whispered. "They look sort of dull."

"They're cute," Mrs. Lewis mused. "But Mollie is more the showy type."

"Heather certainly deserves a lot of credit for helping Mollie," Cindy pointed out, applauding furiously as Mollie turned around at center stage.

From the back of the auditorium she heard the whistles and cheers of her own friends mixed with the loud shouts of approval from Mollie's group. A wide grin flashed across Mollie's serious features just before she ducked behind the curtain.

The show ended a short time later. Cindy weaved her way through the crowd in search of her friends. She found them outside the school enjoying the bright sunshine.

"Thanks for coming," she said, slipping her arm around Grant's waist. "I know it must've been tempting to take off for the beach."

"We wanted to show Mollie that we still care," Grant said, ruffling Cindy's hair affectionately.

Anna nodded in agreement. "From a distance, she's not such a bad kid."

"It was our pleasure," Duffy chimed in, looking more like his devilish self. "Besides, we figured your mom would be putting on a feast afterward."

Cindy laughed. "You figured right. And she's invited all of you to join us."

"Anyone interested in Moveable Feasts chow should hot-foot it over to my Trans Am on the double!" Grant proclaimed jubilantly, punching his fist into the air.

Everyone darted off toward the school parking lot, leaving Grant and Cindy in their wake.

Grant shook his head and laughed.

"What are we waiting for?" Cindy asked in confusion, tugging at the sleeve of his white polo shirt.

"We're waiting for Duffy to remember that we drove over here in that old beater of his, not in my car." Grant shoved his hands into the pockets of his jeans and rocked on his heels.

"They may end up searching the entire parking lot," Cindy scolded. "This is just the kind of joke Duffy would pull."

"I know, Cindy," Grant said with a huge smirk. "I know."

"Great party, huh?" Cindy asked, poking her head into Mollie's bedroom later that evening.

Mollie, sprawled on the bed with a pen and a tablet of pink paper, looked up and smiled. "The greatest."

"Can I come in?" Cindy asked.

"Sure," Mollie invited.

Cindy sat on the edge of the mattress and looked down at Mollie's tablet. "Are you doing your homework?"

"Heck, no. Not on good paper like this!"

"You really looked super in your blue dress

today," Cindy said sincerely. "I'm glad everything worked out."

Mollie nodded, chewing thoughtfully on the tip of her pen. "Everything did work out, didn't it? I've got my old friends back. And I can go back to doing all the things I like to do best. I wasn't sure there for a while what was right for the two of us," she admitted.

Cindy nodded, tracing her finger around the rose appliqué on Mollie's bedspread. "I know what you mean. We're not used to being just two. When Nicole took off for Boston, it sort of felt like a third of me was suddenly torn away," she confessed.

"Exactly," Mollie agreed, her blue eyes full of understanding. "Clinging to each other seemed like the natural thing to do. How were we to know that sisters can overdose on togetherness?" She blurted out with a laugh.

"Especially sisters as different as we are," Cindy added, smiling.

"It was interesting for me to see how the other half lives," Mollie said. Then, with sudden inspiration, she added, "Say, Cindy, maybe you'd like to tag along with my crowd sometime, just to see what it's like."

Cindy shook her head. "No, thanks," she declined in an adamant tone. "I only go to the mall when I really need to buy something."

"Sometimes you can be such a bore," Mollie teased.

"And sometimes you can be such a nutcase," Cindy shot back.

Mollie grinned. "I was just writing a letter to

Nicole," she said, tapping her pen on the bright pink tablet. "I thought I'd tell her about what's been going on during the last few weeks. Why don't we write it together?"

"Okay, shrimp. Good idea. What have you got so far?" Cindy asked, glancing down at the paper.

Mollie looked up sheepishly. "Dear Nicole."

Mollie looked up at Chuck, suppressing a sigh. No wonder she was in love with him—he was so handsome. "Listen, Chuck, I was thinking. We really didn't have time on Saturday to take a look at the beach. I know this great place—a lookout point, sort of. How would you like to ride over there after school today?"

"Oh, I don't think ..." Chuck said, and then stopped, looking down at Mollie as she struggled to keep her disappointment from showing on her face. "Well," he said slowly, "if it means that much to you ... yeah, I guess I can make it, for a little while, anyway."

"Oh, Chuck, that's terrific!" Mollie exclaimed, suppressing the urge to put her hand on his arm. "I know you'll like this place—it's my very favorite spot." She was so excited at the thought of the two of them going to the beach together to watch the sun set that she could hardly contain herself.

The afternoon sun was just as gloriously romantic as Mollie had remembered it, and as she and Chuck parked their bikes at the overlook and locked them, she shivered a little with anticipation. It was all working out exactly as she'd hoped. Here they were, together, alone, on the most romantic point along the entire Santa Barbara coastline just as the sun began its long descent toward the western horizon. To the north swept the soft, clean sands unbroken by rocks; to the south, jagged cliffs tumbled down to the sea, the waves breaking around them with a constant, muted roar. Along the shoreline, the gulls dipped and whirled, and an occasional pelican swept low along the waves, looking for a fishy snack.

"Hey, this is pretty neat!" Chuck said appreciatively. He wandered over to the edge and looked down. "Can we get down there? Down to that big rock, I mean? It looks like a perfect place to sit."

"Sure," Mollie said confidently. She started down the little path that led to the rocky ledge twenty feet below. Once there, they sat down, side by side, and leaned against the sun-warmed rock. Mollie closed her eyes and tried to calm the nervous flutter in her stomach. It was such a beautiful spot: private, secluded, *romantic*. Did Chuck feel the tug of romance as strongly as she did? Would he hold her hand? Would he ... would he kiss her? Mollie's heart executed a triple somersault at the dizzying thought of his arm around her shoulders, his lips coming closer to hers—

Chuck nudged her sharply with his elbow. "Hey, Mollie, what's that?"

Mollie sat up and opened her eyes. Chuck was peering through a pair of binoculars at something far out at sea.

"What's what?"

He handed her the binoculars and pointed. "See? Out there? It looks like a tower or something."

"Oh, that," Mollie said. "That's just an oil rig. There are lots of them around here."

"Oh," Chuck said. He put the binoculars back to his eyes and began to scan the horizon again, as Mollie leaned against the warm rock and closed her eyes, giving herself once again to her imagination. Chuck's arm around her shoulders, his lips coming closer to hers, his voice soft and gentle and caressing—

"Hey, wow!" Chuck shouted excitedly. "There's a *whale* out there! I just saw it spout!"

Mollie opened her eyes again. "Yeah," she said, "they

hang around here sometimes. People go out on charter boats to look at them."

Chuck stood up and pulled a field guide out of his pocket. "Listen, I'm going to walk down to the beach and see if I can identify some seashells and stuff," he said. "But you look so comfortable dozing there in the sun that I don't want to disturb you. Stay where you are—and if I'm not back in about ten minutes, go on home without me. I'll find my own way back."

And with a pat on her shoulder and a quick grin, he was gone.

For a minute, Mollie looked after him, her mouth dropping open. And then she shut her mouth, her lips drawing together in a tight line. So much for a soft, lovely sunset. So much for romance. A half hour later, she stood up. She was bored with watching the whales spout, her rear end ached from sitting on the hard rocks, and it was obvious that Chuck wasn't coming back before dark. She climbed the path, unlocked her bike, and rode home. There was a giant, aching lump in her throat and it hurt to swallow.